THE
DESPERATE
PEOPLE

Francis Durbridge

WILLIAMS & WHITING

Cover design by Timo Schroeder

9781912582716

Williams & Whiting (Publishers)
15 Chestnut Grove, Hurstpierpoint,
West Sussex, BN6 9SS

Titles by Francis Durbridge published by Williams & Whiting

Murder At The Weekend – the rediscovered newspaper serials and short stories

Also published by Williams & Whiting:
Francis Durbridge : The Complete Guide
By Melvyn Barnes

Send For Paul Temple Again

The Doll

The Female of the Species (The Girl from the Hibiscus and Introducing Gail Carlton)

The Man From Washington

The Passenger

The World of Tim Frazer

Tim Frazer and the Salinger Affair

Tim Frazer and the Mellin Forrest Mystery

INTRODUCTION

Francis Durbridge (1912-98) was the most popular writer of mystery thrillers for BBC radio from the 1930s to the 1960s. As early as 1938 he found the niche in which he was to establish his name, when his radio serial *Send for Paul Temple* was a great success and his subsequent radio serials over several decades built an impressive UK and European fanbase. So it was natural that, while continuing to write for radio, he should join the rush of writers into the newer medium of television.

The Desperate People was his tenth BBC television serial, transmitted in six thirty-minute episodes from 24 February to 31 March 1963, although it could legitimately be defined as his twelfth because its immediate predecessor *The World of Tim Frazer* consisted of three interlinked serials of six episodes each. The producer and director, Alan Bromly, had been since 1955 the guru for most of the Durbridge television serials, just as Martyn C. Webster had been for Durbridge's radio serials from the 1930s to the 1960s.

The Durbridge/Bromly television partnership had made an excellent start with *Portrait of Alison* in 1955, and they cemented their relationship by consistently thrilling viewers with all the Durbridge elements that became so familiar – numerous red herrings, cliff-hanger endings to each episode, and the certainty that viewers should not believe anything anyone says. *The Desperate People* maintained this tradition, with some of Durbridge's most enticing cliff-hangers.

Durbridge fans had been enthralled by these features from his television debut, *The Broken Horseshoe* (1952), and throughout his subsequent serials *Operation Diplomat* (1952), *The Teckman Biography* (1953/54), *Portrait of Alison* (1955), *My Friend Charles* (1956), *The Other Man* (1956), *A Time of Day* (1957), *The Scarf* (1959) and *The World of Tim Frazer*

(1960/61). He had become firmly established as the pre-eminent exponent of the thriller serial on UK television, the master of the twisting plot following the tortuous trail of a protagonist in a vicious web spun by a killer who remained concealed until the final episode. And there was always the special factor of "Britishness" to distinguish Durbridge thrillers from the numerous American imports of television crime series to the UK – a quality, incidentally, that also applied to another UK television dramatist who was admired by Durbridge and was his nearest rival, Nigel Kneale, who created Professor Quatermass in horrifying science fiction serials.

The BBC repeated *The Desperate People* from 3 August to 7 September 1963, but it took until 2016 for a DVD to be marketed - included in the box set *Francis Durbridge Presents Volume 1*, BBC/Madman, 2016. And the title of the set *Francis Durbridge Presents* is itself significant, defining an important aspect of his television career – because Durbridge's success in television drama was monumental, with the result that for all his serials from 1960, beginning with *The World of Tim Frazer*, the BBC gave him the unprecedented accolade of the "*Francis Durbridge Presents*" screen credit before the title sequence of each episode.

In spite of his Britishness, or perhaps because of it, Durbridge built an enormously popular career in Europe. His radio serials were broadcast in various countries from the late 1930s, in translation and using their own actors; and beginning with *The Other Man* (1959 in Germany as *Der Andere*) there was a swell of European television versions that attracted a large body of viewers. So addictive was Francis Durbridge on both radio and television in Germany that commentators defined his serials as *straßenfeger* (street sweepers) because a huge proportion of the population stayed at home to listen to them on the radio or watch them on television. And in the case of *The Desperate People*, the German television version was *Die Schlüssel* (18 – 22 January 1965, three episodes), translated by Marianne de Barde and adapted and directed by Paul May; and the Polish television version was *Desperaci* (26 September – 10 October 1974, three episodes), translated by Kazimierz Piotrowski and directed by Anna Minkiewicz.

Durbridge radio and television serials were also popular when adapted as cinema films, although it must be admitted that by the time of *The Desperate People* this had long dwindled (not enough explosions, car chases and sex, perhaps?). Here, however, it is worth recording that his cinematic reputation was earlier established by the films *Send for Paul Temple* (1946), *Calling Paul Temple* (1948), *Paul Temple's Triumph* (1950), *Paul Temple Returns* (1952), *The Broken Horseshoe* (1953), *Operation Diplomat* (1953), *The Teckman Mystery* (1954), *Portrait of Alison* (1955) and *The Vicious Circle* (1957). But sadly the film world appears to have lost interest in Durbridge after the 1950s, whereas his radio and television careers proceeded apace.

Returning to his 1963 television serial *The Desperate People*, it was a perfect demonstration of the skills that made his name on both radio and television. It had, as always, a superb cast – including, in his first and only role as a Durbridge protagonist, the distinguished actor Denis Quilley (1927-2003). But a surprise for today's viewers is that a thorough villain was played by Nigel Hawthorne (1929-2001), who later appeared in numerous television roles but perhaps most notably as Sir Humphrey Appleby in *Yes, Minister* and *Yes, Prime Minister* throughout the 1980s.

As with many of Francis Durbridge's radio and television scripts, *The Desperate People* was novelised – published by Hodder & Stoughton in March 1966. So typical of novelisations, there were plot and/or character changes for the printed page; and this time the name of the central character was changed from Larry Martin to Philip Holt, and his dead brother's name from Philip Martin to Rex Holt. But the plot remains faithful to the original, and it subsequently appeared in Germany as *Der Schlüssel*, in Italy as *I disperati*, in the Netherlands as *De laatste* uitweg and in Poland as *Desperaci*. And fortunately for those who like audiobooks, there is a reading by Neil Pearson on six CDs (AudioGO, 2013).

Melvyn Barnes
Author of *Francis Durbridge: The Complete Guide* (Williams & Whiting, 2018)

This book reproduces Francis Durbridge's original script together with the list of characters and actors of the BBC programme on the dates mentioned, but the eventual broadcast might have edited Durbridge's script in respect of scenes, dialogue and character names.

THE DESPERATE PEOPLE

A Serial in Six Episodes
By FRANCIS DURBRIDGE
Broadcast on BBC Television 24 February – 31 March 1963
Produced and Directed by Alan Bromly
CAST:

Philip Martin	Philip Guard
Andy Wilson	Barry Jackson
Man in street	Brian Proudfoot
Larry Martin	Denis Quilley
Ruth Sanders	Renny Lister
Model	Valerie Stanton
Taxi driver	Steve Kirby
Douglas Talbot	Garard Green
Arthur	Artro Morris
Vanessa Curtis	June Ellis
Dr Linderhof	Gerard Heinz
Doreen	Rosemary Rogers
Det-Insp Hyde	Hugh Cross
Woman with pram	Thelma Holt
Postman	Stanley Walsh
Thomas Quayle	David William
Woman at accident	Diana Oxford
Policeman	Tony Poole
Policeman	Peter Thornton
Det-Sgt Macey	Stuart Hutchison
Clare Seldon	Shirley Cain
Det-Insp Lang	Peter Ducrow
Model girl	Yvonne Antrobus
Nurse	Leonie Forbes
Cliff Fletcher	Nigel Hawthorne
Ticket seller	Hugh Lund
Cloakroom Attendant	Edward Brooks

Luther Harris .Stanley Meadows
Peggy Grahame . . . . Frances Collier
Norman Stansdale . . . . John Flint
Freda Stansdale . . . . Hilary Crane
Singer . . . . Pam Reece
Eddie Meadows . . . . Clifford Earl
Det-Sgt Harrison . . . . Colin Pinney
Police Sergeant . . . . William Kendrick
Oscar Naylor . . . . Kenneth Keeling
Joyce Naylor . . . . Janet Davies
Police Sergeant . . . . Frank Dunne
Sgt Wainwright . . . . Michael Hunt
Sgt Bellamy . . . . Desmond Cullum-Jones

EPISODE ONE

OPEN TO: Liverpool Street Station.

Arrivals are giving up their tickets at the barrier as they leave the platform. Among them are two uniformed soldiers – privates in the British Army. PHILIP MARTIN, eager, boyish looking, in his middle twenties – and ANDY WILSON, stocky, cheerful, a few years older than his friend. Both are carrying kit-bags; PHILIP also carries a small suitcase, ANDY a zip-bag. They are laughing and talking together as they move away from the barrier. PHILIP slings down his kit-bag for a moment's respite, slapping ANDY on the shoulder as they say goodbye. As ANDY hurries off, PHILIP smiles after him, then hoists his kit-bag on his shoulder to the exit.

CUT TO: A busy thoroughfare near Liverpool Street Station.

PHILIP MARTIN appears and makes to cross the road at a busy junction. A car turns the corner just as PHILIP steps onto the roadway. With great presence of mind, PHILIP quickly retreats, moving back onto the pavement. The car continues down the road. PHILIP stares after it – his expression a mixture of anger and relief. The incident is over in a second. It is difficult to know whether it was a deliberate attempt to run him down or not.

CUT TO: A Mews in Knightsbridge.

A taxi drives up and stops outside the main entrance to LARRY MARTIN's flat. PHILIP MARTIN gets out of the car, complete with luggage. There is a showcase on the wall near the entrance door. The case bears the name: LARRY MARTIN – and includes photographs of several professional models, a well known film star, and a head and shoulders photograph of PHILIP, uniformed and smiling. The TAXI DRIVER stares at the showcase as PHILIP searches his pockets for change.

CUT TO: The Living Room of LARRY MARTIN's Flat. This is a first floor mews flat. A composite set, comprising living room, hall, front door, photographic studio and bedroom. The living room has doors leading to the hall and other rooms. LARRY MARTIN is a professional photographer and his work is much in evidence in this large and tastefully furnished room. Along with books on photography in the well-filled bookshelves are stacked photographs, mostly unframed. There are framed photographs on the wall – mostly of models advertising various beauty products, beachwear, winter sports clothes etc.

Seated at a small, cluttered desk, tucked away in a corner of the room, LARRY's secretary, RUTH SANDERS, is typing a letter. RUTH is an intelligent and efficient girl in her late twenties. She stops typing, rises, and opens the top drawer of a nearby filing cabinet. The drawer contains photograph proofs. RUTH is searching through these when LARRY MARTIN enters from the studio. He is strong-featured; casually dressed but with no suggestion of obvious artiness. LARRY is serious about his work at a photographer, but is also down-to-earth about it, with no artistic pretensions.

LARRY: Have you heard from my brother?

RUTH: No.

LARRY: (*Anxiously glancing at his watch*) He should have been here an hour ago.

RUTH: It's only a quarter to twelve – if the train was half an hour late that only allows him twenty-five minutes from Liverpool Street.

LARRY: (*Smiling*) Yes, of course …

RUTH: Don't worry, he'll turn up! (*Crossing to her desk*) How did you get on with the dumb blonde?

LARRY: She wasn't so dumb after all.

RUTH: I am surprised!

The door bell rings.

4

LARRY: She damn nearly told me how to take the pictures.

The door bell continues to ring.

LARRY: … It's all right, I'll answer it.

LARRY turns and goes out into the hall. He opens the front door and PHILIP is in the doorway.

LARRY: Phil!

PHILIP: Larry!

LARRY: Phil – at last! I thought you were never going to get here! (*Puts his arms around his brother's shoulders*) It seems ages, Phil …

As they cross the hall towards the main room.

LARRY: How are you? How have you been keeping? Did you have a good journey?

PHILIP: Yes, fine. Why, hello, Ruth! You look wonderful!

RUTH: Thank you. Nice to see you, Phil.

LARRY and PHIL move into the main room. PHILIP crosses to RUTH and kisses her.

LARRY: I say, what's the idea – kissing my secretary?

PHILIP: British Army, old boy – special privileges.

RUTH laughs and taking out a file from the desk goes out into the studio

PHILIP: Now let's take a good look at you! (*He stands back and looks at his brother*) You look tired, Larry. Have you been overdoing things?

LARRY: Yes: I've been trying to clear the decks so we can see a little of each other during the next three weeks.

PHILIP: Well, I hope you succeeded. Last time I was on leave, I couldn't drag you out of that blasted studio.

LARRY: Yes, I know.

PHILIP: (*Feeling his collar*) Larry, I must get out of this uniform, it's driving me nuts.

5

LARRY: (*Nodding towards the bedroom*) Your things are ready for you – including that monstrosity of a sports jacket …

PHILIP: (*Laughing*) Nonsense!

LARRY: Anyway there's plenty of time. Have a drink first.

PHILIP shakes his head and, crossing to the settee, starts to unbutton his tunic: during the following dialogue he slowly unlaces his boots and partly undresses.

PHILIP: Larry, I'm afraid I've a bit of a disappointment. I've got to go over to Dublin for two or three days.

LARRY: (*Surprised*) Dublin?

PHILIP: Yes, I'm catching the 3.15 this afternoon. But with a bit of luck I'll be back on Thursday – Friday at the latest.

LARRY: (*Puzzled*) But – what on earth are you going to Dublin for?

PHILIP: Oh, it's a nasty business. A lousy job, in fact. I wish to God I hadn't got to go.

LARRY: Why? What's happened?

PHILIP: Larry, did I ever mention a chap to you called Reynolds – Sean Reynolds?

LARRY: Sean Reynolds?

PHILIP: Yes: he was with me when I first went to Germany. An awfully nice chap. Irish. Talked a hell of a lot – never stopped talking.

LARRY: (*Thoughtfully*) I seem to remember something about him. You were in trouble over a late-night pass and he …

PHILIP: That's it – that's the chap! He fixed it. He could fix anything could dear old Sean.

He takes a wallet out of his pocket and a postcard-size photograph out of the wallet.

PHILIP: Anyway, to cut a long story short, he's dead. He was killed in a car accident about ten days ago.

LARRY: Oh, good Lord! Where was this?

PHILIP: In Hamburg. We'd been to a show one night – a whole party of us. Sean was in pretty high spirits, and just as we left this place he started to fool about on the sidewalk. The poor devil stepped off the kerb just as a whacking big car came racing round the corner. The driver slammed his brakes on but there was just nothing he could do: nothing any of us could do, it was over in a matter of seconds.

LARRY: Was he killed instantly?

PHILIP: No, they rushed him into hospital. He died twenty-four hours later. I went to see him the morning after the accident. He was conscious, and oddly enough didn't seem to be in a great deal of pain. But I think he knew he was going to die, Larry. Just as I was leaving he gave me his wallet and asked me if I'd go over to Dublin and see his wife.

LARRY: (*Quietly*) I see.

LARRY looks at the photograph. It is of a man in Army uniform and a woman in a cocktail dress. The woman is holding an accordion, her hands on the keyboard. She is a good-looking woman in her early thirties. The man is leaning over his wife, hands resting on her shoulders. Both are looking straight into the camera and smiling.

LARRY: (*Looking up*) Have you met his wife?

PHILIP: No.

LARRY: (*Returning the photograph*) She's a good-looking woman.

PHILIP: Yes. Sean used to talk about her – never stopped talking about her, in fact. Andy Wilson and I used to pull his leg about it.

LARRY: Have they any children?

7

PHILIP: No, thank goodness. Oh, God, Larry – it's a lousy business. (*Puts the photograph and wallet in his pocket*) I wish I didn't have to go.

LARRY: You say you're catching the 3.15?

PHILIP: Yes. From St Pancras.

LARRY: Well, there's loads of time. Let's have a drink.

LARRY crosses to the drinks cabinet.

PHILIP: I shan't stay longer than is necessary. If all goes well, I'll be back on Thursday.

LARRY: I'm going to a dinner on Thursday night, and I'm afraid I can't very well get out of it.

PHILIP: That's all right, Larry, don't worry about that. I've still got the key you gave me. If I'm late I'll let myself in. I shall probably be dead beat, anyway.

LARRY: (*At cupboard*) What would you like – a beer?

PHILIP: I'd like a gin and tonic if you've got one.

LARRY: One gin and tonic, coming up! How's Andy Wilson these days?

PHILIP: Oh, he's fine. We travelled up to town together. Which reminds me, don't fix anything for the 29th – I'm going to a dance with Andy.

LARRY: That'll be nice.

PHILIP: (*Laughing*) I'm not taking him, you idiot! I shan't be long. I'm just going to change.

PHILIP goes toward the bedroom.

LARRY: Phil …

PHILIP turns.

LARRY: … if you must wear that terrible jacket – not the yellow tie, please …

PHILIP grins and goes into the bedroom. LARRY mixes the drinks.

CUT TO: The Mews.

A taxi drives up, stopping outside of LARRY MARTIN's flat. The TAXI DRIVER gets out looking up at the building and moves to the flat entrance. He rings the doorbell. He glances idly at the showcase on the wall near the entrance. This is the case we have seen before with LARRY's name above it and various photographs of PHILIP, uniformed and smiling. The TAXI DRIVER is more interested in the glamour study of the film star. PHILIP and LARRY come out of the flat entrance. LARRY is carrying PHILIP's suitcase. PHILIP is now wearing a rather loud check sports jacket and dark flannel trousers.

TAXI DRIVER: Mr Martin?

LARRY: Thank you.

LARRY gives the TAXI DRIVER the suitcase and they move towards the cab. PHILIP gets in.

PHILIP: See you Thursday then, Larry.

LARRY: (*Nodding*) Let me know if there's anything you want.

PHILIP: Yes, I will, of course. Thanks. (T*o the DRIVER*) St Pancras, please.

The DRIVER nods.

PHILIP: Bye, Larry …

LARRY waves a hand as the taxi drives off.

CUT TO: *The taxi pulls up outside the glossy, West End showroom of a car rentals firm. PHILIP gets out. The DRIVER mutters drily as PHILIP feels in his pocket.*

TAXI DRIVER: I thought you wanted St Pancras.

PHILIP: (*Curtly*) I changed my mind. How much?

TAXI DRIVER: Four and a tanner on the clock.

PHILIP: Thanks.

PHILIP pays him and picks up his suitcase and goes into the office of the car rentals firm.

CUT TO: A road sign which indicates that traffic is now entering Maidenhead.

The camera pans back to take in a Morris Minor driving towards the road sign. We see that the driver is PHILIP. He is alone in the car.

CUT TO: The exterior of the Royal Falcon Hotel, Maidenhead. It is a fairly luxurious riverside hotel on the outskirts of Maidenhead.

PHILIP's Morris Minor draws up outside the hotel.

CUT TO: The Reception Desk and Hall of the Royal Falcon Hotel.

From behind the reception desk, DOUGLAS TALBOT, the hotel manager, is talking to ARTHUR, a melancholy porter of about fifty.

TALBOT: I've told Miss Jessop you'll take her poodle for a walk – so when you have a moment, Arthur …

ARTHUR: (*With obvious reluctance*) Yes, all right, Mr Talbot …

TALBOT takes some new magazines from near the letter rack and gives them to ARTHUR.

TALBOT: And you might take these into the lounge, Arthur.

PHILIP arrives at the reception desk, carrying his suitcase.

TALBOT: (*To ARTHUR*) And remove some of the older ones.

ARTHUR goes and TALBOT automatically turns on the extra charm reserved for new faces at the hotel. His smile freezes slightly on seeing PHILIP's sports jacket.

TALBOT: Good afternoon, sir. (*More a question than a greeting*)

PHILIP: Good afternoon.

PHILIP smiles pleasantly, although his manner is slightly different from that of his earlier scenes. His boyishness has gone. He is more serious and preoccupied.

PHILIP: I believe you have a reservation for Mr Philip Martin?

TALBOT consults his visitors book. His manner is distant.

TALBOT: Yes, we have; but I'm afraid Mr Martin hasn't arrived yet.

PHILIP: (*Unsmiling*) I'm Mr Martin.

TALBOT is obviously taken aback.

TALBOT: You telephoned this morning asking for a room with a bath?

PHILIP: (*Correcting him*) I asked for one of your best rooms.

TALBOT hesitates.

TALBOT: It'll be three guineas a night, sir – for the room only.

PHILIP: (*Unsmiling*) You'd like me to pay in advance?

TALBOT: (*Hastily*) Er, no, no of course not. But I thought … would you sign the book, please?

He turns the book around to PHILIP and offers his pen. PHILIP takes the pen, looks at TALBOT, still unsmiling, and signs the book.

TALBOT: Have you any idea how long you'll be staying with us, Mr Martin?

PHILIP: (*Handing back the pen*) Three or four days. Certainly until Thursday morning.

VANESSA CURTIS, the owner of the hotel, enters. She goes to the letter rack. She is a smart, attractive woman of about thirty. She smiles at PHILIP.

VANESSA: Good afternoon.

PHILIP: Good afternoon.

VANESSA takes letters from the rack, selecting those addressed to her. TALBOT fetches a key and calls ARTHUR who is just coming out of the lounge.

TALBOT: Arthur …

PHILIP: By the way, I'm expecting a parcel. Has it arrived yet?

TALBOT: I don't think so, Mr Martin.

He looks under the desk. VANESSA moves to a drawer, opening it.

VANESSA: Some arrived just before lunch. I put them in here.

TALBOT: Oh, thank you, Mrs Curtis.

TALBOT looks through the parcels.

VANESSA: You haven't stayed with us before, Mr Martin?

PHILIP: No – no, I'm afraid I haven't.

VANESSA: Well – I'm sure you'll enjoy your stay.

PHILIP: Thank you – I hope so.

TALBOT: Here we are, Mr Martin.

He hands Philip a small parcel.

PHILIP: Thank you.

VANESSA goes as PHILIP looks at the parcel. TALBOT hands ARTHUR the key and indicates PHILIP's suitcase.

TALBOT: Number 27, Arthur …

ARTHUR nods and takes up the suitcase. PHILIP is opening the parcel: he has taken the paper off, revealing a book. He looks thoughtfully at the title. We see that it is called: "Sonnets and Verse" by Hilaire Belloc. PHILIP looks thoughtfully at the book)

CUT TO: The lounge of the Royal Falcon Hotel. It is two days later.

VANESSA CURTIS stands at a wall table arranging flowers in a bowl. DR WOLF LINDERHOF is seated nearby, glancing through the final pages of a magazine. He is a rather

12

tired looking man in his late fifties. He speaks with a slight accent.

VANESSA: … Arthur tells me you went to the theatre last night, Dr Linderhof?

LINDERHOF: (*Looking up*) Yes, I did … to the Old Vic. It was most enjoyable. (*Holding up magazine*) This is an interesting magazine, Mrs Curtis. I haven't seen it before.

VANESSA: It's American. My husband used to take it, and after he died I kept up the subscription. I've only just put this month's copy on the table.

LINDERHOF: Ah … good. Thank you.

He goes to the magazine table. PHILIP is seated in an armchair near this table. He is still wearing the sports jacket and is reading the book of poems by Hilaire Belloc. Without looking he takes a packet of cigarettes from his pocket and opens it. The cigarettes slip from the packet and in his attempt to catch them PHILIP drops the book. LINDERHOF turns and picks up the book whilst PHILIP collects the fallen cigarettes.

PHILIP: Thank you.

LINDERHOF glances at the title of the book as he hands it back to PHILIP.

LINDERHOF: Poetry …?

PHILIP makes no comment.

LINDERHOF: Not many people read poetry nowadays, I'm afraid.

PHILIP: (*Unsmiling*) No … I suppose not.

LINDERHOF: (*Friendly*) You like Hilaire Belloc?

PHILIP: (*Puzzled*) Hilaire … (*Suddenly*) Yes, I do. (*Curtly*) Very much.

He looks at the book ignoring the doctor. LINDERHOF looks thoughtful, trying to remember something. Suddenly he smiles.

LINDERHOF: (*Quoting from memory*) "Believe too little and go down despairing; Believe too much and lose it at the end. Believe in none and die over-caring; Believe in all and die without a friend".

PHILIP looks up at LINDERHOF, obviously a shade puzzled.

LINDERHOF: That's Belloc. Surely you recognise it? You must have read it many times.

PHILIP: (*Not very convincingly*) Yes. Yes, I have.

He continues reading the book. LINDERHOF stares at PHILIP, puzzled by his manner. VANESSA CURTIS comes to the magazine table and selects a magazine.

VANESSA: Here it is, Dr Linderhof.

LINDERHOF: Oh … thank you.

He takes the magazine, nods to PHILIP, and goes to a nearby chair

VANESSA: (*To PHILIP*) You're leaving us tomorrow then, Mr Martin?

PHILIP: (*Looking up*) I think so … yes.

VANESSA: Well … I hope we'll see you again.

PHILIP: Thank you.

VANESSA: It's a pity you haven't had better weather.

PHILIP: Yes … Yes, it is.

He nods and returns to his book again. VANESSA hesitates, uncertain whether to continue the conversation.

VANESSA: Well, enjoy the rest of your leave.

PHILIP: (*Not looking up*) Thank you.

VANESSA goes. PHILIP continues to read his book. LINDERHOF, with the newly opened magazine on his lap, quietly looks up. He stares in PHILIP's direction with a faintly puzzled air. He is wondering why PHILIP didn't recognise the lines he quoted.

CUT TO: A service room in the Royal Falcon Hotel. It is the morning after.
DOREEN, a maid, is preparing a breakfast tray. She looks tired and irritable. ARTHUR enters the room carrying a pair of shoes he has just cleaned.
ARTHUR: Mornin', Doreen.
DOREEN: (*Curtly*) Hello …
ARTHUR: Shoes for Number 14 …
DOREEN: I only got one pair of hands, you know.
ARTHUR: All right, all right …
DOREEN: I didn't sleep a wink last night! What a racket!
ARTHUR: It was a twenty-first party.
DOREEN: I thought they were going on all night! And then all those flipping cars racing off at two in the morning …
ARTHUR: You're only young once, Doreen. (*Indicating tray*) Who's this for?
DOREEN: Young chap in twenty-seven …
ARTHUR hands DOREEN the shoes and takes up the tray.
ARTHUR: Take it easy, duckie.
He goes out with the tray. DOREEN slaps the shoes down on the table, muttering to herself)

CUT TO: A corridor at the Royal Falcon Hotel.
Arthur arrives at the door of room number 27 carrying the tray. He knocks and enters the room closing the door behind him. He moves to the bed, then stops, staring at the pillow end of the bed. The tray falls from his hands. PHILIP is lying in bed, motionless, his hands outside the covers. His right hand, limp on the pillow, is still holding the revolver pointed at his head. ARTHUR remains there, stupefied with shock. His eyes

15

flicker towards the bedside table; something on it has attracted his attention. It is a white envelope with the handwritten address on it: Larry Martin Esq., 29 Melton Mews, London, S.W.1.

CUT TO: The same – later.

LARRY is standing near the bed, looking towards DETECTIVE INSPECTOR HYDE. LARRY looks tense and worried. HYDE is in his late forties; a shrewd, determined looking man. VANESSA CURTIS is also in the room, and ARTHUR, the porter, stands quietly bewildered near the door. The body of PHILIP MARTIN has been removed. LARRY is holding the note that was in the envelope.

LARRY: "Dear Larry, Please forgive me – but this is the only way out. Phil" … It's my brother's handwriting, there's no doubt about that. (*Shaking his head, confused*) But I don't know what the note means … what Phil was referring to …

HYDE: I should have thought it was obvious, Mr Martin.

LARRY: (*On edge*) It might be obvious to you, Inspector … it certainly isn't obvious to me!

VANESSA: The Inspector means that your brother was in trouble and committed suicide.

HYDE nods.

LARRY: Yes, well, I'm sorry, Mrs Curtis, but I'm not prepared to accept that explanation. I just don't believe that Phil did commit suicide.

HYDE: Look, Mr Martin, I can quite appreciate how you feel. This business has been a shock to you … a terrible shock … on the other hand you've got to face the facts, and the facts are …

16

LARRY: The facts are, if Phil had been in trouble …
           serious trouble … he'd have told me about it!
HYDE: But he didn't tell you about it, sir! That's just
           the point. He lied … he told you he was going
           to Dublin.
LARRY: I … I think he'd every intention of going to
           Dublin.
HYDE: (*Surprised*) You mean, he changed his mind?
LARRY: Yes.
HYDE: Why?
LARRY: I … I don't know why.
HYDE: (*Quietly*) Mr Martin, I believe the story
           you've told me; the story about your brother
           and Sean Reynolds and the car accident …
           but the fact remains there's nothing to
           substantiate that story. I've been through your
           brother's belongings; there's no wallet,
           there's no photograph.
LARRY: But he had the wallet, and the photograph …
           he showed them to me.
HYDE: (*Shaking his head*) He hasn't got them now,
           sir.
VANESSA: Mr Martin, when you saw your brother on
           Monday morning did he mention this hotel
           and the possibility of his staying here?
LARRY: No, of course he didn't! He said he was going
           to Ireland.
VANESSA: Well, that proves he wasn't telling the truth,
           doesn't it?
LARRY: What do you mean?
VANESSA: This room was booked before he saw you …
           he telephoned from Harwich early on
           Monday morning. Mr Talbot, my manager,
           took the call and made the reservation.

17

LARRY stares at VANESSA, obviously impressed by what she said, but not wishing to believe her.

HYDE: Anyway, we can take it you didn't know your brother was coming here, sir, and you haven't the slightest idea why he came?

As LARRY nods in confirmation the INSPECTOR turns towards VANESSA.

HYDE: Now what exactly did Mr Martin do during his stay at the hotel, Mrs Curtis? Did he have any visitors or telephone calls?

VANESSA: No, he kept very much to himself. He spent most of the time reading, didn't he, Arthur?

ARTHUR: Yes; he was always reading. (*Indicating the book on the table*) The moment that book arrived he buried 'is head in it … never took it out so far as I could see …

LARRY: (*Surprised*) But Phil never read a book from one year's end to the next! A magazine perhaps or …

HYDE moves down to the table.

ARTHUR: He read that one all right. He was always readin' it, wasn't he, Mrs Curtis?

VANESSA: Well, whenever I saw him he certainly was.

HYDE picks up the book.

HYDE: (*To Arthur*) You said: the moment the book arrived. Didn't he bring it with him, then?

ARTHUR: No, I don't think so. (*He looks at VANESSA*)

VANESSA: It was posted to him. The parcel was here, waiting for Mr Martin.

HYDE: Did he ask for it?

VANESSA: Yes.

LARRY: (*To HYDE*) What is the book?

The INSPECTOR looks at the title.

18

HYDE: It's a book of poems, sir. "Sonnets and Verse" by
           Hilaire Belloc.
LARRY: Are you serious?

*He crosses and, taking the book from HYDE, stares at the
title.*

LARRY: Phil never read this! Not in a thousand years! ...

CUT TO: The living room of LARRY MARTIN's flat.
*RUTH is sitting at the desk typing a letter; she finishes the
letter and is taking it out of the typewriter when she hears the
opening and closing of the front door. As RUTH turns LARRY
enters from the hall. He looks tired and dejected as he takes
off his hat and coat.*

RUTH: Hello, Larry! You had me worried. I expected you
           ages ago.

RUTH takes LARRY's hat and coat.

LARRY: I meant to phone but I just didn't get round to it.
           Are there any messages?
RUTH: Nothing important. Oh – Andy Wilson phoned.
           He's in London; he's going to call round.
LARRY: He knows, I suppose?
RUTH: Yes. But he didn't know until this morning. He's
           been staying down in Cornwall with an aunt of
           his.

LARRY nods.

RUTH: He was awfully upset, Larry.
LARRY: Yes; I imagine he was.
RUTH: What happened this morning – at the inquest?
LARRY: (*Bitterly*) Suicide – without sufficient evidence to
           show the state of mind of the deceased ...
RUTH: (*Quietly*) You don't think it was suicide, do you,
           Larry?
LARRY: (*Almost turning on her*) I'm damn sure it wasn't!
           Why should Phil commit suicide?

19

RUTH: I don't know. But perhaps he had a reason, something we know nothing about. It isn't always clear why people do these things.

RUTH looks at Larry; concerned.

RUTH: Did you have anything to eat this morning?

LARRY: No.

RUTH: I'll get you something.

The doorbell rings.

LARRY: No, I don't want anything. I don't feel like eating … (*turns towards the hall*) It's all right, Ruth. I'll see who it is.

LARRY returns to the hall and opens the front door. HYDE is in the doorway; he carries the book of poems.

HYDE: Hello, Mr Martin. I think we missed each other this morning. May I come in?

LARRY: Yes – yes, of course.

HYDE enters the hall and then he and LARRY go through to the living room.

LARRY: This is Miss Sanders – my secretary. Inspector Hyde …

HYDE: Good afternoon, Miss Sanders.

RUTH: Good afternoon, Inspector.

RUTH continues working at the desk.

HYDE: I thought I'd have a word with you, sir, because I've been making a few enquiries since we last met.

LARRY: About my brother?

HYDE: About the story he told you, sir. I'm sorry, Mr Martin, but that story of your brother's wasn't true, it was pure fabrication.

LARRY: What do you mean?

HYDE: We've been in touch with his regiment, sir. We've talked with several of his colleagues.

LARRY: Well?

HYDE: There wasn't a car accident in Hamburg. The man
           your brother mentioned – Sean Reynolds – didn't
           exist.

LARRY: (*Astonished*) He didn't exist?

HYDE: No, sir.

LARRY: What the hell do you mean, he didn't exist? I saw
           a photograph of him with his wife. Phil showed
           me the photograph!

HYDE: Your brother may have shown you a photograph,
           sir ...

LARRY: <u>May</u> have shown me a photograph? He did show
           me a photograph!

HYDE: Well, all I can say is; we didn't find it, sir – or the
           wallet. (*Changing the subject*) Mr Martin, I've
           brought you the book your brother was reading.
           It's been to the labs – there's nothing special
           about it. It's just an ordinary book.

LARRY takes the book.

LARRY: It may be an ordinary book to you. Inspector, but
           I just can't believe my brother spent two days
           reading it.

HYDE: Well, apparently he did, sir. I've made extensive
           inquiries. He spoke to hardly anyone in the hotel;
           he spent most of his time reading.

LARRY: I just can't believe that, I refuse to believe it! (*To
           RUTH*) Do you believe it, Ruth? Phil reading a
           book of poems?

RUTH: It certainly doesn't sound like Phil.

*RUTH comes and takes the book from LARRY and looks at
the title.*

HYDE: (*To LARRY*) Incidentally, we've spoken to the taxi
           driver – the chap you saw. Your brother apparently
           changed his mind about St Pancras five minutes
           after leaving here.

The doorbell rings.

LARRY: What does that prove?

HYDE: Well, since he'd already phoned Car Rentals it proves, to my mind at any rate, that he'd never any intention of going to St Pancras.

RUTH looks up, hearing the doorbell, and goes out into the hall, putting the book down on the desk as she goes.

LARRY: You say Phil had already telephoned – about the car?

HYDE: Yes; he phoned Car Rentals from Harwich. He'd already made arrangements about the car when he told you that cock and bull story about catching the 3.15 to Dublin.

LARRY quietly; puzzled but impressed.

LARRY: Are you sure about this?

HYDE: I'm quite sure, sir.

Voices are heard in the hall. RUTH returns with ANDY WILSON. ANDY is in uniform and carries the zip-bag.

ANDY: Larry …

LARRY: Hello, Andy …

ANDY: Larry, this is terrible … I just don't know what to say … When I heard it, I – I just couldn't believe it.

LARRY: No, I don't think any of us could.

LARRY pats ANDY on the arm and is turning away when he realises that HYDE is looking at ANDY.

LARRY: Oh, this is Inspector Hyde … (*to HYDE*) This is Andy Wilson. He's a … He was a friend of my brother's.

HYDE: (*Nodding*) Good afternoon, sir. (*To LARRY*) I'll say goodbye, Mr Martin.

LARRY: Goodbye, Inspector.

HYDE moves towards the hall then hesitates.

HYDE: (*Turning*) Oh – Mr Wilson?

ANDY: Yes, sir?

HYDE: Does the name Sean Reynolds mean anything to you?

ANDY: No, I'm afraid it doesn't.

HYDE looks at LARRY.

HYDE: You've never heard it before?

ANDY: No, sir. (*Puzzled*) Should I have done?

HYDE ignores the question and addresses LARRY again.

HYDE: Goodbye, Mr Martin. I hope we shall meet again some time – under pleasanter circumstances.

HYDE nods to ANDY and follows RUTH out into the hall.

ANDY: (*To LARRY*) What was he talking about, Larry? Who's this chap, Sean Reynolds?

LARRY: Phil told me a story about a man called Sean Reynolds. He said he'd been killed in a car accident. It was a most convincing story – he even showed me a photograph of him.

ANDY: (*Puzzled*) Well?

LARRY shakes his head; there is a touch of bitterness in his voice. The INSPECTOR has obviously convinced him.

LARRY: It wasn't true. It just wasn't true, Andy.

ANDY: Look, Larry – I'm sorry, I don't know what this is all about … But one thing I do know. (*He looks at LARRY*) I don't believe Phil committed suicide. (*Shaking his head*) I just don't believe it.

LARRY: (*Quietly*) No. Neither do I …

CUT TO: Exterior of LARRY MARTIN's flat.

ANDY WILSON, carrying his zip-bag, comes out of the flat. He hesitates as he passes the showcase on the wall. We see the showcase from ANDY's viewpoint as he looks at it; the smiling photograph of PHILIP. ANDY's expression saddens as he stares at the photograph. After a moment he moves on

... ANDY walks briskly out of the mews into the main thoroughfare.

CUT TO: A quiet, tree-lined street in Knightsbridge.
ANDY is walking along. He makes up his mind to cross the street, hesitates, waiting for a car to pass. We see the passing car from ANDY's viewpoint. The nearside, rear window is open. Just as the car has passed a hand appears in the open window holding an automatic. ANDY steps into the road, the car having passed him. Three shots ring out in rapid succession. ANDY staggers, dropping the zip-bag. He reels to one side, clutching his shoulder. He staggers towards the pavement, collapsing onto it. There is the sound of running feet, and the shrill scream of a woman from across the street.

CUT TO: The front door of LARRY MARTIN's flat. *HYDE appears, carrying his hat and overcoat, and presses the doorbell. He stands quietly waiting for the door to be opened.*

CUT TO: The hall and living room of LARRY MARTIN's flat.
LARRY crosses the hall and opens the front door. He is a shade surprised to find the visitor is HYDE.
HYDE: Good evening, Mr Martin. May I have a word with you?
LARRY: Yes, of course. Come in.
HYDE enters the hall. He then goes into the living room followed by LARRY. He puts his hat and overcoat down on a chair near RUTH's desk.
LARRY: Can I get you a drink?
HYDE: No, thank you, sir. Mr Martin, what time was it when Mr Wilson left you this afternoon?
LARRY: (*Surprised by the question*) What time?

24

HYDE: Yes.

LARRY: It was about four o'clock; it might have been ten past, it certainly wasn't any later.

HYDE: He stayed with you about twenty minutes, then?

LARRY: (*Puzzled*) That's right.

HYDE: Did he say where he was going when he left?

LARRY: Yes: he said he was going down to Aldershot. He has an appointment there tomorrow morning.

HYDE: (*Nodding*) How long have you known Mr Wilson, sir?

LARRY: About a year. My brother first introduced us ... I say, what is this? Why all these questions about Andy Wilson? Has something happened to him?

HYDE: Yes; I'm afraid it has, sir. Shortly after leaving here Wilson was shot.

LARRY: Shot?

HYDE: Yes. He's in the Middlesex Hospital at the moment. On the danger list, I'm afraid.

LARRY: But this is unbelievable! I mean ... Who shot him?

HYDE: We don't know, sir. The shots were fired from a car. He was crossing Felton Street at the time.

LARRY: You say he's badly hurt?

HYDE: Yes; it's very serious, I'm afraid, sir. (*Suddenly changing the subject*) Mr Martin, when I was here this afternoon, I left that book with you – the one your brother was reading.

LARRY: Yes.

HYDE: (*Quietly*) I'd like to take another look at it, if I may, sir?

LARRY: (*Quietly: puzzled*) Yes, of course.

LARRY crosses to the bureau, obviously expecting to find the book on top of the desk. It isn't there. He opens the desk and looks inside: still not finding the book he commences to search the drawers.

25

HYDE: (*Watching him*) I don't think you'll find it, Mr
               Martin.

LARRY: (*Turning*) What do you mean?

*HYDE crosses to the chair and takes the book of poems out of
his overcoat pocket. LARRY stares at the book in
astonishment.*

HYDE: (*Quietly: watching LARRY*) Yes, sir.

LARRY: Well – how did you get it?

HYDE: It was in the zip-bag that Andy Wilson was
               carrying.

*LARRY moves down to where HYDE is standing. The
telephone rings.*

LARRY: You mean – Andy took the book?

HYDE: He must have done, sir. Unless you gave it to
               him. (*Shaking his head*) And you obviously
               didn't, Mr Martin.

*LARRY stares at HYDE, bewildered and unbelieving, then he
turns and still looking at the INSPECTOR picks up the
telephone receiver.*

LARRY: (*On phone*) Hello? … Yes, speaking …
               Who? … Oh, just a minute, please … (*To
               HYDE*) It's for you – Sergeant Harris.

HYDE: (*Nodding and quickly taking the receiver*)
               He's at the hospital. (*On phone*) Hyde
               speaking … Yes … Yes, go on, Sergeant …
               When was this? … Is he still delirious? … I
               see … No; no don't do that, Sergeant – stay
               where you are. I'll keep in touch … Thank
               you for ringing. (*Replaces receiver*)

LARRY: (*Tensely*) What's happened?

*HYDE moves away from the desk, deep in thought. He looks
at LARRY.*

HYDE: About half an hour ago Wilson became
               delirious; he started talking. He mentioned

26

	someone called Larry. I imagine he meant you, Mr Martin.
LARRY:	Well?
HYDE:	(*Still looking at LARRY*) He said: "Larry – destroy the photograph."
LARRY:	Destroy the photograph?
HYDE:	Yes.
LARRY:	Which photograph? Which photograph did he mean?
HYDE:	I don't know, sir. I'm only repeating what he said.
LARRY:	(*A note of tenseness*) Do you think he meant the photograph I told you about? The Sean Reynolds photograph – the one Phil showed me?
HYDE:	I don't know, Mr Martin. (*Politely*) In any case, you haven't got that photograph, have you, sir?
LARRY:	No. No, you know I haven't. Phil took it away with him, I told you that.

LARRY stares at HYDE, bewildered and confused.

| LARRY: | He said … "Larry, destroy the photograph? … ? |
| HYDE: | Yes, that's right, sir. (*Quietly; still looking at him*) That's what he said, Mr Martin … |

CUT TO: The Mews. Day.
A POSTMAN is walking along the mews. The showcase cannot be clearly seen.

CUT TO: The living room of LARRY MARTIN's flat.
The telephone is ringing. LARRY comes out of the bedroom, coffee cup in hand. He puts the cup down and crosses to the telephone.

LARRY: (*On phone*) Hello? … Yes – speaking … Oh,
              hello, Mr Turner! … I think we sent the
              proofs off to you last night … I'll check with
              my secretary as soon as she comes in and get
              her to ring you back … Thank you, Mr
              Turner.

*LARRY replaces the receiver and the front doorbell rings. He
turns and goes out into the hall and opens the front door. The
postman stands there glancing through a bundle of letters and
a large envelope.*

POSTMAN: (*Without looking up*) Morning, sir …
LARRY: Good morning. More bills, by the look of
              them.

*We hear the sound of RUTH's heels as she hurries up the
stairs from the main entrance.*

POSTMAN: Martin … Martin … that's the lot, I think.
LARRY: Thank you.

*As LARRY takes the letters and the large envelope, RUTH
hurries into shot.*

RUTH: (*Breathlessly*) Good morning.
LARRY: (*Smiling and accentuating the "morning"*)
              Good morning, Ruth.
RUTH: Phew! Sorry I'm late.

*RUTH enters the hall and LARRY closes the door and follows
her into the living room.*

RUTH: I'm awfully sorry about this morning, Larry,
              but I've got a very good excuse …
LARRY: (*Smiling*) You overslept.
RUTH: (*Laughing*) That's right.
LARRY: (*Opening the big envelope*) Don't worry I'm
              late myself this morning. Oh, by the way,
              Turner telephoned. He wants you to give him
              a ring.
RUTH: Is anything the matter?

28

LARRY: The proofs haven't arrived.

RUTH: I posted them. I posted them last night.

LARRY: Well, have a word with him.

RUTH crosses to the desk and, removing her gloves, picks up the telephone book. LARRY turns his attention to the opened envelope. He draws out a large photograph. We do not see it for the moment.

LARRY: (*Softly surprised*) What the devil's this? Where did this come from?

RUTH looks up, puts down the telephone book, and crosses to LARRY.

LARRY: (*Indicating photograph*) This has just arrived …

LARRY hands RUTH the photograph. We now see that it is a photograph of LARRY's brother PHILIP, an identical photograph to the one in the showcase outside the flat)

RUTH: Who sent it?

LARRY: I don't know. There was no letter … as far as I know.

RUTH takes up the envelope and looks at it.

RUTH: No – no, there's nothing here.

LARRY: Why should someone send me a photograph of Phil? I don't understand this, Ruth … (*He turns over the photograph and looks at the back of it*) It's one of my own photographs, too. I took this …

RUTH: (*Interrupting him*) Yes, it's the same as the one in the showcase downstairs.

LARRY: That's right. I took it about six months ago when Phil was … (*He stops*) The showcase? (*He stares at Ruth, then looks at the photograph again*) My God, I wonder …

29

LARRY suddenly rushes out into the hall; we hear the front door bang. RUTH stares after him, then looks down bewildered at the envelope in her hand.

CUT TO: The entrance to the flat. We can just see the edge of the showcase.
LARRY comes out of the flat and looks up at the showcase. LARRY stares in amazement at the showcase. He looks down at the photograph in his hand. As he raises his head once more the camera pans upwards to the showcase. The photograph of PHILIP has been replaced by another photograph. It is the photograph of SEAN REYNOLDS and his wife.

END OF EPISODE ONE

EPISODE TWO

OPEN TO: The living room of LARRY MARTIN's flat. *Present are LARRY MARTIN, RUTH SANDERS and DETECTIVE INSPECTOR HYDE. LARRY is holding the photograph of SEAN REYNOLDS and his wife that he found in the showcase. The photograph of his brother PHILIP that he was sent is on the side.*

LARRY: (*Indicating the photograph of PHILIP*) I felt sure this photograph of Phil was the one out of the showcase so I went down to take a look.

HYDE: (*Indicating the photo LARRY has in his hand*) And you found this?

LARRY: (*Nodding*) Yes.

HYDE: Is this the photograph you told me about, the one your brother showed you?

LARRY nods. He passes the photograph he is holding to HYDE who looks at it; studying it.

HYDE: Mr Martin, would you mind telling me your story again, from the beginning?

LARRY: My brother – Phil – was with the B.A.O.R. in Germany and came home on leave. I thought he was going to stay with me the whole time – the full three weeks – but when Phil arrived here he told me that a service friend of his, an Irishman called Sean Reynolds, had been killed in a car accident in Hamburg. He said that he'd promised the dead man that he'd go over to Dublin and see his wife. He showed me a photograph of Mr and Mrs Reynolds.

LARRY indicates the photograph in HYDE's hand.

LARRY: That photograph.

HYDE: (*Quietly*) I see.

LARRY: The rest you know. Phil didn't go to Dublin – instead he went to Maidenhead.

HYDE: And committed suicide.

LARRY: (*Shaking his head*) I don't think he did commit suicide, Inspector.

HYDE: Then what do you think happened to him?

LARRY: I think he was murdered.

HYDE: (*Politely*) And who do you think murdered him, Mr Martin?

LARRY: I don't know. But just for the record, Inspector – I'm going to find out.

HYDE looks at LARRY.

HYDE: Mr Martin, I've spoken to the authorities in Hamburg; to several of your brother's colleagues, and last night I had a word with his Commanding Officer. (*Shaking his head*) There was no car accident in Hamburg. No one's heard of Sean Reynolds.

RUTH: Then who are the people in the photograph?

HYDE: I don't know.

HYDE looks at RUTH. There is a twinkle in his eye.

HYDE: But just for the record, Miss Sanders – I'm going to find out.

CUT TO: The exterior of the Royal Falcon Hotel. *LARRY's car draws up outside the hotel. LARRY gets out of his car and moves to the hotel entrance.*

CUT TO: VANESSA CURTIS's room at the Royal Falcon Hotel.

It is a small, tastefully furnished room on the ground floor of the hotel. There are several vases of nicely arranged flowers, several mirrors, pretty cushions – it is obviously a room occupied solely by a woman. There is nothing particularly feminine about the desk, however. It is large and littered with ledgers, hotel menus, a portable typewriter and a small tray containing tea things.

34

VANESSA CURTIS is seated at this desk, just finishing the pouring of a cup of tea. At the same time, she is going through a pile of bills, making mental calculations. She makes a note of the final figure on a writing pad. There is a knock at the door.

VANESSA: Come in!

DOUGLAS TALBOT enters.

TALBOT: I'm sorry to trouble you, but Mr Martin is here.

VANESSA: Larry Martin?

TALBOT: Yes.

VANESSA: (*Rising*) Ask him to come in.

TALBOT nods and goes, leaving the door open. VANESSA looks quickly in the direction of the mirror to make sure she is presentable. TALBOT returns almost immediately, showing LARRY in.

VANESSA: Good afternoon, Mr Martin.

TALBOT goes, closing the door behind him.

LARRY: Good afternoon. I hope I haven't called at an inconvenient time?

VANESSA: Not at all.

LARRY: Mr Talbot said you were busy …

VANESSA: I'm afraid one is never anything else in this business. Do sit down …

LARRY: (*Crossing to an armchair*) Thank you.

VANESSA: Would you care for a cup of tea?

LARRY: Er – no thank you, Mrs Curtis.

VANESSA sits at her desk, turning her chair towards LARRY.

VANESSA: Well – what can I do for you?

LARRY: I don't know whether you've read the papers about a young man called Andy Wilson?

VANESSA: Andy Wilson? No, I don't think so …

LARRY: He was shot – yesterday afternoon.

VANESSA: Shot?

35

LARRY:	Yes; he was crossing a road in Knightsbridge. Someone fired at him from a passing car. He's in the Middlesex Hospital, very seriously ill, I'm afraid.
VANESSA:	(*Puzzled*) Was this young man a friend of yours?
LARRY:	He was a friend of my brother's. They were in the Army together.
VANESSA:	Oh. Oh – I see.
LARRY:	Mrs Curtis, I'll be quite frank with you. I don't think my brother committed suicide; I think he was murdered.
VANESSA:	Murdered?
LARRY:	Yes.
VANESSA:	And you think the attempt on this young man's life …?
LARRY:	(*Nodding*) I think the attempt on Andy's life was – in some unaccountable way – connected with the death of my brother.
VANESSA:	Do the police think that?
LARRY:	I don't really know what the police think; but I've got a shrewd suspicion that they're not quite as happy as they were. Mrs Curtis, I wonder if you would be kind enough to give me the names and addresses of all the people who were staying here at the time of my brother's death?
VANESSA:	(*After a momentary hesitation*) Yes, I can get Talbot to do that, certainly. But most of the people were known to me, you know. Apart from your brother I think there was only one stranger in the hotel – Dr Linderhof.
LARRY:	Dr Linderhof?
VANESSA:	Yes.

LARRY: That's a German name.

VANESSA: (*Nodding*) Yes; he is German.

LARRY: What was he doing here, do you know?

VANESSA: I think he's been ill, and he was resting. He was a quiet, rather charming little man. I liked him enormously.

LARRY: How long did Dr Linderhof stay with you?

VANESSA: About a week. He left this morning.

LARRY: For Germany?

VANESSA: Yes. For Hamburg, I believe.

LARRY: Do you happen to know whether my brother spoke to Dr Linderhof at all?

VANESSA: (*Shaking her head*) Your brother never spoke to anyone. As I told the Inspector, he kept completely to himself. I'm sorry I can't be more helpful, Mr Martin.

The door opens and THOMAS QUAYLE enters. He is VANESSA's brother. He is a tall, languid, fastidiously dressed man in his late thirties. He carries a small white dog which, like THOMAS, is well groomed.

THOMAS: Vanessa darling, I've been talking to that temperamental manager of yours and he tells me … (*Noticing LARRY*) Oh, I beg your pardon!

VANESSA: Come in, Thomas. This is Mr Martin. (*To Larry*) My brother – Thomas Quayle.

As LARRY rises, THOMAS crosses and shakes hands with him.

THOMAS: How do you do, Mr Martin? I'm delighted to meet you. I saw your Fleet Street exhibition last year – enjoyed it enormously.

LARRY: Thank you.

THOMAS: Vanessa, I'm sorry to disturb you; I'll drop in later.

LARRY:	It's all right, Mr Quayle, I'm just leaving. (*To VANESSA*) You'll let me have that list, Mrs Curtis?
VANESSA:	Yes, I will.
THOMAS:	I was very sorry to hear about your brother – a most distressing affair. It must have been a terrible shock for you.
LARRY:	Yes, it was.
THOMAS:	I understand you were under the impression he was in Ireland?
LARRY:	Yes, he told me he was going there.
THOMAS:	How very odd. (*Stroking his dog*) Are you preparing another exhibition, Mr Martin?
LARRY:	No. I've been doing a lot of work for the advertising agencies. They've kept me pretty busy recently.
THOMAS:	Yes, I'll bet they have.
LARRY:	What's your line, Mr Quayle? Are you in the hotel business?
THOMAS:	God forbid! I leave that headache to Vanessa and our dear friend Talbot. I have a small antique shop in Arundel. It's not exactly Mallett's but it keeps me out of mischief. (*To the dog*) Doesn't it, Whitie?
VANESSA:	(*Irritated by her brother*) I'll come down with you, Mr Martin.
LARRY:	Thank you. (*To THOMAS*) Goodbye …

THOMAS nods, smiles at LARRY, and stands gently stroking the dog.

CUT TO: The exterior of the Royal Falcon Hotel. *ARTHUR, the porter, comes out of the hotel entrance carrying several small pieces of luggage. He takes them to a stationary car. LARRY comes out of the entrance and crosses down to his own car. ARTHUR puts down the luggage and approaches LARRY.*

ARTHUR: Oh – excuse me, sir.

LARRY hesitates at the door of his car. ARTHUR joins him, fumbling in his pocket.

ARTHUR: Doreen – the maid, that is – found a key in your brother's room this morning.

ARTHUR produces the key and hands it to LARRY.

LARRY: Oh – thank you.

ARTHUR: I think it must have been your brother's, sir, because we …

LARRY: Yes, it is. Actually, it's my front door key. I lent it to my brother. Thank you very much.

ARTHUR nods and opens the door of LARRY's car. LARRY gets in.

LARRY: Thanks again. Goodbye.

ARTHUR: Goodbye, sir.

ARTHUR touches his forehead and closes the car door. The car starts and moves away.

CUT TO: The front door of LARRY MARTIN's flat. *LARRY arrives at the door, taking the key from his pocket. He makes to insert it in the lock. It doesn't fit. He looks at the key, faintly puzzled. The door is suddenly opened by RUTH.*

RUTH: Oh, it's you, Larry!

LARRY looks at RUTH.

LARRY: (*Abstractedly*) I was using the wrong key …

RUTH: (*Smiling*) I thought someone had got the wrong flat.

LARRY looks at the key again, then puts it in his pocket and enters the hall. RUTH closes the door.

RUTH: There's a Dr Linderhof waiting to see you.

LARRY is taking off his hat and coat and hesitates on hearing LINDERHOF's name.

LARRY:	Dr Linderhof?
RUTH:	Yes. Were you expecting him?
LARRY:	No.
RUTH:	He's been waiting almost an hour. I told him you might be some time but he insisted on waiting.
LARRY:	(*Nodding, quietly*) Yes, all right, Ruth.

LARRY and RUTH move through into the living room. DR LINDERHOF is studying one of the many photographs on the wall.

LARRY:	Dr Linderhof?
LINDERHOF:	(*Turning*) Ah, Mr Martin!
LARRY:	I'm sorry to have kept you waiting, Dr Linderhof.
LINDERHOF:	Not at all. It's entirely my fault. I should have telephoned for an appointment. (*Smiling*) But I've enjoyed myself, looking at your excellent work.

LARRY indicates the settee.

LARRY:	Sit down, doctor.

LINDERHOF crosses to the settee.

LINDERHOF:	Thank you. Mr Martin, I've been staying at the Royal Falcon Hotel. I was there when your brother … died.
LARRY:	Yes, I know.
LINDERHOF:	I'm sorry, Mr Martin, but I don't think the Coroner's verdict was a correct one. I don't think your brother did commit suicide.
LARRY:	Then what do you think happened, Dr Linderhof?
LINDERHOF:	I don't know what happened, but I'm sure it wasn't suicide. The night before your brother died, I was not feeling too well. I have an ulcer and sometimes it is troublesome,

especially during the night. On this particular night I had to go along the corridor to the bathroom. The bathroom was next to Room 27 – the room your brother occupied.

LARRY nods.

LINDERHOF: I'd been in the bathroom for about five minutes when I suddenly realised that your brother was talking to someone. He sounded tense, excited. I heard him say, "I'm going back to London … I'm not spending another minute reading that book and waiting for that friend of yours."

LARRY: Go on, doctor …

LINDERHOF: I heard a woman say, "If I were you I'd wait – even if it means staying here the rest of the week." Your brother said: "I'm not waiting a day longer and that's final …"

LARRY: Who was this woman – did you recognise her voice?

LINDERHOF: (*After a momentary hesitation*) Yes, I'm afraid I did.

LARRY: Well, who was it?

LINDERHOF: It was Mrs Curtis.

LARRY: Are you sure about this?

LINDERHOF: (*Nodding*) Quite sure.

LARRU: Did you hear anything else, doctor?

LINDERHOF: No. No, I was embarrassed. I made a point of not listening. After a little while I went back to my bedroom.

RUTH moves down from the desk. She is interested in what the doctor is saying.

RUTH: What time was this, doctor?

LARRY turns towards RUTH.

LINDERHOF: I said it was night just now – but it was morning, of course: about half past one.

RUTH: Half past one?

LINDERHOF: Yes.

LARRY: Just eight hours before they found Phil?

LINDERHOF: Yes.

LARRY looks at RUTH.

LARRY: Have you told the police about this?

LINDERHOF: No.

LARRY: Why not?

LINDERHOF: Mr Martin, I'd better be honest with you. I didn't go to the police because I don't want any publicity at the present moment. (*Nervously shaking his head*) In fact, I mustn't have any, otherwise … (*Hesitates; then:*) Next week I'm appearing before a Medical Tribunal in Hamburg. If things go badly for me, I doubt if I shall be allowed to practice medicine ever again.

LARRY: Oh – I'm sorry to hear that.

LINDERHOF: A patient of mine has made certain allegations. False allegations, I assure you, but I won't bore you with the details, Mr Martin. However, believe me, at this moment I'm in a very, very difficult situation. That's why I came to England. I wanted to rest. I wanted to prepare myself for whatever is going to happen to me.

LARRY: I see.

LINDERHOF: Now if you'll excuse me. I'm catching the seven o'clock plane.

LARRY: There's nothing else you can tell me, Dr Linderhof – about my brother, I mean?

LINDERHOF: Nothing. I've told you everything I know. There is nothing else, Mr Martin, except …

LARRY: Yes?

LINDERHOF: Except that if you repeat this within the next few days, I hope you won't mention my name. (*With a shrug*) After next week it won't matter one way or the other. (*Turning towards RUTH, smiling with a little bow*) Auf Wiedersehen.

The telephone starts to ring.

RUTH: Goodbye, doctor.

LINDERHOF and LARRY cross towards the hall. RUTH watches them, still intrigued by the doctor's story, then she turns and answers the telephone.

RUTH: (*On the phone*) Hello?

VANESSA's VOICE: Can I speak to Mr Larry Martin, please?

RUTH: Who is it speaking?

VANESSA's VOICE: Mrs Curtis.

RUTH: (*Surprised*) Oh – just hold on a moment, will you?

RUTH puts down the receiver and turns towards the hall as LARRY returns from showing out Dr LINDERHOF.

RUTH: It's Mrs Curtis …

LARRY looks at RUTH, obviously surprised. He crosses to the telephone. RUTH watches him during his conversation with MRS CURTIS.

LARRY: (*On phone*) Mrs Curtis? Larry Martin here …

VANESSA's VOICE: (*Pleasantly*) Oh, Mr Martin, I believe Arthur gave you a key this afternoon. The stupid man thought it was your brother's.

LARRY: Yes, we both made a mistake, I'm afraid.

VANESSA's VOICE: Well, would you be kind enough to post it back to me? It's mine – and it's rather important.

LARRY: If it's important, Mrs Curtis, I'd sooner deliver it. In any case, I want to see you again.

VANESSA's VOICE: Oh, really? What is it you want to see me about?

LARRY: My brother …

VANESSA's VOICE: But we discussed your brother this afternoon …

LARRY: (*Interrupting her*) We did. We did indeed. But I don't think you were quite as frank with me as you might have been. For one thing – you didn't tell me why you went to Phil's room the night he was murdered.

VANESSA's VOICE: (*Taken aback; softly*) I – I didn't go to his room.

LARRY: I think you did, Mrs Curtis.

VANESSA's VOICE: Who have you been talking to? Who's been telling you lies about me …

LARRY: Mrs Curtis, I'm sorry, but much as I'd like to discuss this subject, we can't discuss it on the phone. I suggest we meet tomorrow.

VANESSA's VOICE: (*After a moment*) All right …

LARRY: I'll see you at the hotel.

VANESSA's VOICE: (*Tensely*) No, don't come to the hotel. (*A moment*) Do you know a café in Datchet called "Hobson's"?

LARRY: "Hobson's"?

VANESSA's VOICE: Yes, it's near the Castle.

LARRY: I don't – but I can find it.

VANESSA's VOICE: I'll see you there tomorrow morning. We – we can talk then, Mr Martin.

LARRY: All right.

44

VANESSA's VOICE: Eleven o'clock.

LARRY: I'll be there.

VANESSA's VOICE: And please – don't forget the key. (*She rings off*)

LARRY looks thoughtfully at the receiver and then replaces it.

RUTH: What did she say?

LARRY: (*His thoughts still on the conversation*) I'm seeing her tomorrow morning.

The doorbell rings.

RUTH: Where – at the hotel?

LARRY: No, she's asked me to meet her at a café in Datchet.

RUTH: But why not at the hotel?

LARRY: I don't know.

RUTH: What's happened, Larry, when you suggest that … (*She stops and turns towards the hall*) That's the door …

LARRY looks towards the hall.

LARRY: Have I an appointment?

RUTH: No.

LARRY: Well, see who it is. I don't want to see anyone unless it's important.

RUTH nods and goes out into the hall. LARRY, deep in thought, crosses to the settee. He takes a cigarette from the box on the table and is about to light it when RUTH returns.

RUTH: A Mr Quayle would like to see you. (*Puzzled*) He says you met this afternoon at Maidenhead.

LARRY: Yes, we did. (*Nodding towards the telephone*) It's her brother.

RUTH: Mrs Curtis?

LARRY: Yes. What's he want, do you know?

RUTH: (*Shaking her head*) He just says he'd like a word with you. (*Smiling*) He's got a sweet little dog with him.

45

LARRY: All right, Ruth – ask him in.

RUTH returns to the front door. LARRY is lighting his cigarette when RUTH shows in THOMAS QUAYLE. THOMAS wears a little overcoat, an exaggeratedly neat bowler hat, and carries the dog.

THOMAS:Mr Martin, this is really unforgivable, dropping in like this – but I was on my way back to Arundel and I thought …

LARRY: That's all right, Mr Quayle. Nice to see you again. Oh, this is my secretary, Miss Sanders.

THOMAS: How do you do?

RUTH nods to THOMAS and strokes the dog.

RUTH: Isn't he sweet?

THOMAS:He's a darling, isn't he? (*To the dog*) Whitie, say hello to Miss Sanders. (*The dog struggles*) Now don't be stupid, Whitie … Whitie … (*Laughing*) It's extraordinary, isn't it? It's always the same when you want them to behave …

LARRY: Can I offer you a drink?

THOMAS: No; no thank you. It's really most kind of you, Mr Martin, but I can't stay. (*Smiling*) I just dropped in to collect my key.

LARRY: Your key?

THOMAS:Yes, Arthur gave it to you this afternoon by mistake. What the silly little man was thinking of I can't imagine. I told him several days ago that I'd lost my key and to be on the lookout for it.

LARRY: The key was found in Room 27, so I suppose he thought …

THOMAS:He thought it was your brother's. Yes, of course. A   natural mistake, under the circumstances. (*To RUTH*) Poor Arthur doesn't exactly scintillate at the best of times. (*To dog*) Does he, Whitie? (*Holding out his hand*) Well, if you'll give me my

46

key, Mr Martin, I won't take up any more of your valuable …

LARRY: (*Also smiling; interrupting*) I'm sorry, but I'm afraid I can't do that.

The smile fades from THOMAS's face.

THOMAS: What do you mean?

LARRY: I haven't got the key. When I arrived home, I discovered the mistake and immediately posted it back to your sister.

THOMAS: (*Not quite sure how to take this*) Oh – oh, I see.

LARRY: So all you've got to do is ring up Mrs Curtis – and no doubt she'll send it on to you.

THOMAS: Yes, yes, of course. (*The smile returns*) Well – once again, my apologies.

LARRY: That's all right. Are you sure you won't change your mind about the drink?

THOMAS: Yes, I'm quite sure. (*To dog*) Say goodbye to Miss Sanders, Whitie.

RUTH strokes the dog and goes towards the hall with THOMAS.

RUTH: Do you live in Arundel, Mr Quayle?

THOMAS: I have an antique shop in Roedean Crescent. Do you like Arundel?

RUTH: Yes, I do – quite.

THOMAS: I adore it.

They go out. LARRY turns his back on them and moves down to the settee. He takes the key out of his pocket and looks at it.

CUT TO: Datchet High Street

LARRY is crossing the road.

CUT TO: A street in Datchet. It is the scene of an accident. *A POLICEMAN is kneeling beside an injured person who is out of frame at the moment. They are surrounded by a group*

47

of onlookers. LARRY turns the corner, approaching the scene. He hesitates momentarily. He then moves quickly forward. The POLICEMAN rises.

POLICEMAN: Stand back now, please. Stand back …

LARRY joins the onlookers staring down at the injured person. It is a man. He is holding his leg, obviously in pain. LARRY looks relieved. He turns to the woman next to him.

LARRY: What happened?

WOMAN: I didn't see it. The car had gone when I came out of the café.

POLICEMAN: (*Overhearing*) He won't get far. Chap here got his number for us.

WOMAN: Must've been drunk, I should think; coming up on the pavement like that. The woman was lucky.

LARRY looks at her.

LARRY: Woman?

WOMAN: Yes – going straight for her it was … so they said. She looked terrible. They was just taking her into the café when I came out.

LARRY goes quickly out of shot. The WOMAN stares after him.

CUT TO: A CAFÉ in Datchet.

LARRY enters, looking quickly around. He reacts to seeing VANESSA CURTIS who is seated at a table. Near her is SERGEANT MACEY, a plain clothes detective. A uniformed POLICEMAN stands beside him. A WAITRESS puts down some coffee on the table as LARRY reaches it.

MACEY: (*To POLICEMAN*) You've got the lady's address?

POLICEMAN: Yes, sir.

MACEY: (*To VANESSA*) Now you're quite sure you wouldn't like us to get hold of a doctor?

VANESSA: (*Tensely; trying to control herself*) Yes, I'm quite sure. I feel perfectly all right now.

LARRY: (*Quietly*) Good morning, Mrs Curtis.

VANESSA looks up. SERGEANT MACEY turns towards LARRY.

MACEY: Are you the gentleman she's expecting, sir?

LARRY: Yes.

MACEY: Sergeant Macey.

LARRY nods.

MACEY: I'm afraid you friend's had rather a nasty experience.

LARRY: (*Looking at VANESSA*) Yes, so I gather. What happened, exactly?

MACEY: Mrs Curtis was on the pavement coming towards the café. A car suddenly got out of control and nearly knocked her down.

LARRY: Did the car stop?

MACEY: No, it didn't.

POLICEMAN: It's my bet the swine was tight and was too frightened to stop.

MACEY looks at LARRY: his look indicates that he doesn't completely agree with the POLICEMAN.

MACEY: Yes, well, we've got his number, so we'll probably pick him up. (*To VANESSA*) Now if you're sure you're all right, Mrs Curtis, we'll be getting along.

VANESSA: Yes, I'm quite all right now. Thank you for being so kind.

MACEY and the POLICEMAN nod to LARRY and cross towards the door. LARRY hesitates, then sits at the table. There is a pause.

LARRY: I should drink your coffee …

VANESSA: (*Not looking at him*) I don't want it.

LARRY:	Would you like me to get you something else?
VANESSA:	(*Shaking her head*) No.

LARRY looks at her; takes out his cigarette case and offers her one. After a moment Vanessa takes one. LARRY takes out his lighter and flicks it. Her hand is shaking. In order to light her cigarette, LARRY has to steady her hand with his own. A pause.

LARRY:	Was it an accident?
VANESSA:	(*Confused*) What?
LARRY:	The car – what happened. Was it an accident?
VANESSA:	(*Agitated*) Why yes, of course. What else could it have been?
LARRY:	It could have been done deliberately. An attempt to frighten you – to stop us from meeting …
VANESSA:	You've got too much imagination, Mr Martin.
LARRY:	Or not enough. (*He looks at her*) I can't imagine what my brother was doing at your hotel, for instance.

VANESSA turns away from him and puts her hand across her eyes.

VANESSA:	I'm sorry, but I don't feel very well. This business with the car has upset me more than I thought … I … (*She rises*) If you don't mind, I'd like to go home.
LARRY:	I'll drive you back to Maidenhead.
VANESSA:	No. No, I've got my car. I'll be perfectly all right.

VANESSA stands holding the table for support, her other hand shielding her eyes.

LARRY:	(*Faintly concerned*) I don't think you ought to drive, Mrs Curtis.

VANESSA: There's nothing to worry about. I shall feel
            better when I'm outside in the fresh air. (*She
            turns towards him holding out her hand*) I think
            you've got my key, Mr Martin.
LARRY: Oh yes. (*Nodding*) Yes, of course.

*LARRY puts his hand in his pocket as if about to produce the
key, then hesitates.*

LARRY: (*Pleasantly, taking his hand out of his pocket*)
            I'm awfully sorry, Mrs Curtis, I seem to have
            forgotten it.

*VANESSA intensely annoyed stares back at him. She knows he
is lying.*

CUT TO: The living room of LARRY MARTIN's flat.
*RUTH is seated at the desk, typing a letter. The telephone
rings. She picks up the receiver.*
RUTH: Larry Martin's studio …

CUT TO: A telephone box in a country lane.
*LARRY is on the telephone. His manner is brisk and business-
like. We cut back and forth between LARRY and RUTH.*
LARRY: Hello, Ruth? Larry here … Listen, I may not
            be back till quite late – so don't wait for me.
RUTH: Did you see Mrs Curtis?
LARRY: Yes, I saw her …
RUTH: (*Curious*) What happened? What did she say?
LARRY: She was in a rather bad way. Just before I
            arrived   someone put the fear of the devil
            into her, so she didn't … I'll tell you about it
            when I see you, Ruth. Are there any
            messages?
RUTH: Inspector Hyde phoned. He didn't leave a
            message; he's ringing back.
LARRY: Yes, all right. Goodbye, Ruth.

RUTH: (*Quickly*) Larry, wait a minute!
LARRY: Yes?
RUTH: Where are you going?
LARRY: (*Amused yet faintly surprised at RUTH's familiarity*) Well, if you must know I'm going down to Arundel to see Thomas Quayle.
RUTH: What are you going to see Quayle for?
LARRY: I'll give you three guesses.
RUTH: (*After a moment, a sudden thought*) You've still got the key …?
LARRY: (*Amused*) Good girl. I'll bring you back a stick of rock. See you later, Ruth.

LARRY replaces the receiver and turns to go out of the telephone box.

CUT TO: An establishing shot of Arundel.

CUT TO: A Street in Arundel.
It's a quiet street with an occasional shop and a few residential flats. The buildings are Victorian with railings at street level and stairs leading down to basement flats. *LARRY's car approaches and draws up at the curb. He gets out and looks up at the building. It is THOMAS QUAYLE's antique shop. LARRY moves to the shop window and looks into it.*

CUT TO: The interior of THOMAS QUAYLE's antique shop.
It is full to capacity with valuable antiques and objects d'art. There are several desks, one containing ledgers, receipts, a desk lamp, and a box of cigarettes: obviously QUAYLE's own desk for conducting his business affairs. At the rear of the shop, partly obscured by furniture, is an alcove which

leads to the basement stairs. These stairs are adjacent to the alcove and cannot be seen from the shop itself.

There is no-one present, but the sound of voices and footsteps ascending the basement stairs are followed by the entrance of CLARE SELDON and THOMAS QUAYLE through the alcove at the rear of the shop. THOMAS is dressed in his customary elegant style, complete with waistcoat and watch-chain. CLARE SELDON is one of those expensively dressed, slightly scatter-brained women who seem to be on an eternal shopping expedition ...

CLARE: ... I don't think I should decide about the nest of tables until my husband's seen them. I know I'm safe with the lamp – I'm sure he'll adore that ...

THOMAS: Well – if your husband is passing perhaps he'd like to drop in and have a look at them himself.

CLARE: Yes, I think perhaps we'll leave it like that. I'll ask him to call in.

THOMAS: Providing, of course, they're still here. We sell that sort of thing very quickly.

CLARE: Yes ... and they <u>are</u> an unusual design, aren't they?

They are moving towards the shop entrance as they talk. THOMAS looks up as LARRY enters the shop.

THOMAS: I shan't keep you a moment – (*Recognising LARRY*) Mr Martin.

LARRY: (*Nodding quietly*) Good afternoon.

CLARE: When can I expect the lamp to be delivered?

THOMAS looks at her blankly for a moment, not having quite recovered from the surprise of seeing LARRY there.

THOMAS: The lamp – yes ... On Wednesday, I should think. Yes – I should be able to manage it then. (*Smiling*) Goodbye, Mrs Seldon.

CLARE: Goodbye. I'll tell my husband to drop in as soon as he can.

THOMAS walks a few paces to the door with CLARE. He opens the door. She smiles at him, hesitates as if about to say something, then goes out. THOMAS slowly closes the door and turns towards LARRY.

THOMAS: To what do I owe this unexpected pleasure, Mr Martin?

LARRY: I'm afraid I owe you an apology. The last time we met I told you that my secretary had posted your key back to Mrs Curtis. Apparently, I made a mistake; she didn't.

THOMAS: You mean she forgot to post it?

LARRY: Yes.

THOMAS: How very odd. Miss Sanders looked such an efficient young lady. However, I was under the impression that you posted it, Mr Martin, not your secretary. (*Indicating chair*) I beg your pardon – do sit down …

LARRY hesitates then sits in the chair near the desk. He is a shade irritated by QUAYLE's manner.

LARRY: I take it you still want the key?

QUAYLE: Of course I do, it's mine. (*Sitting at desk*) If I found a key of yours, Mr Martin, wouldn't you expect me to return it?

LARRY: If I give you this key …

THOMAS: (*Raising his eyebrows*) <u>If</u> you give me the key?

LARRY: Will you give me something in return?

THOMAS: What is it you want?

LARRY: Some information about my brother.

THOMAS: What makes you think I know anything about your brother that you don't already know?

LARRY: I think your sister knew Phil. I think she knew him before he went down to Maidenhead.

THOMAS: (*After a moment, with a shrug*) It's possible. I don't know all my sister's friends, thank

54

goodness. (*Smiling*) I suggest you return my key, Mr Martin, and then have a quiet, cosy little chat with Vanessa.

LARRY: (*Shaking his head*) Your sister's frightened – she refuses to talk to me.

THOMAS: Nonsense! What on earth has Vanessa got to be frightened of?

LARRY: (*Rising*) I think it's about time I brought you up to date, Mr Quayle. I had an appointment with your sister this morning – at a café in Datchet. Shortly before I arrived someone tried to run her down with a car. Fortunately, they failed.

THOMAS rises: he stares at LARRY in astonishment.

THOMAS: Is – is this true?

LARRY nods.

THOMAS: How do you know it wasn't just an accident?

THOMAS is obviously shaken by LARRY's information.

LARRY: (*Watching THOMAS*) I don't think your sister thought it was an accident; but, of course, it could have been.

THOMAS: (*After a moment; quietly*) What is it you want to know about your brother?

LARRY: Was he a friend of yours?

THOMAS: I knew him.

LARRY: You'd met him before he went down to Maidenhead?

THOMAS: (*Quietly*) Yes …

LARRY: Did my brother commit suicide?

THOMAS: (*After a moment; shaking his head*) No. He was murdered.

As THOMAS speaks the shop door opens and CLARE SELDON returns. THOMAS and LARRY turn toward the door. Neither of them has any wish to be interrupted at this particular moment.

CLARE: … Oh, I'm terribly sorry to interrupt, Mr Quayle. (*Smiling*) But I think I'll buy the nest of tables after all. I'm sure my husband will like them.

THOMAS: Very good, Mrs Seldon. We'll send them along with the lamp.

CLARE: If I could just have another peek at them before …

THOMAS: (*Hesitates, then*) Yes, of course. (*To LARRY*) I won't be a minute.

CLARE: (*To LARRY*) I'm awfully sorry; I won't keep him long …

LARRY gives a curt nod. THOMAS and CLARE cross to the alcove and go down into the basement. LARRY, left alone, looks at the various articles in the shop. He notices a chest with a painted lid – a faded reproduction of a Canaletto painting. He glances at the picture on the chest then casually looks at the "sold" ticket attached to the chest. After a moment he crosses and picks up one of a pair of silver candlesticks. He looks at the candlesticks but is obviously disinterested. He is anxiously waiting to continue his conversation with THOMAS. He puts down the candlesticks and strolls casually in the direction of the alcove and the basement stairs. He pauses to look at a writing bureau. There is a bookrest on the bureau: there is a book leaning against it. LARRY moves casually on. He hesitates. A thought strikes him. He turns back to the bureau, taking the book from the bookrest. He looks at the title. It is "Sonnets and Verse" by Hilaire Belloc. Larry stares at the book with mounting curiosity. He turns seeming to hear a sound from the basement. CLARE SELDON's voice is heard as she comes up the stairs.

CLARE's VOICE: All right, then, that's settled.

LARRY quickly replaces the book on the bookrest and moves away, feigning interest in something else.

CLARE's VOICE: And if my husband has any real objection to them – you'll exchange them, then?

THOMAS's VOICE: Yes, of course, Mrs Seldon, of course.

CLARE's VOICE: And I can expect them on Wednesday, along with the lamp?

THOMAS's VOICE: Indeed you can, Mrs Seldon.

CLARE's VOICE: Goodbye, then.

THOMAS'S VOICE: Goodbye, Mrs Seldon.

CLARE SELDON appears through the alcove. She smiles apologetically at LARRY.

CLARE: I'm so sorry to have interrupted you …

LARRY: (*Murmuring*) That's quite all right.

CLARE smiles quickly at him and goes out of the shop. LARRY watches her go, looks quickly in the direction of the alcove, and hearing nothing, moves back to the bookrest. He takes up the book and examines it, glancing from time to time at the alcove, expecting to hear THOMAS coming up the stairs. There is silence. LARRY looks through the pages of the book: then he examines the binding. He looks puzzled. There is obviously nothing extraordinary about the book. The telephone rings. LARRY starts, glancing in the direction of QUAYLE'S desk. He quickly replaces the book and turns away, waiting for the sound of Quayle's footsteps on the stairs. The telephone continues to ring. LARRY turns to look at the alcove. The telephone stops ringing. LARRY stops at the alcove, shrugs lightly, and turns back into the room. He glances idly over the room as he takes out his cigarette and puts it in his mouth. He is about to light it but changes his mind. There is something ominous about the silence below. He goes to the alcove and calls.

LARRY: Mr Quayle? (*Louder*) Mr Quayle?

LARRY listens for a moment, then taking the cigarette out of his mouth goes through the alcove.

CUT TO: The bottom of the stairs in the basement of Quayle's Antique Shop.

The basement room door is padded, giving a foretaste of a luxurious interior.

LARRY comes down the stairs, pausing on the bottom stair to look at the door. He glances back at the stairs, then moves to the door. He raps on it – the sound is muffled by the padding. He decides to call.

LARRY: Mr Quayle?

There is no reply. LARRY looks down at the doorknob. He turns the knob and pushes the door open. The door swings open and LARRY stands in the doorway, looking around the room. There is no-one present. The room, although virtually a cellar, has been tastefully furnished with antiques and many beautiful objects d'art. A door in one wall leads to the stairs leading up to the street. LARRY comes into the room and glances up at the small window through which can be seen a glimpse of the railings above and people walking along the pavement. LARRY's attention moves to a nest of tables: he reflects on CLARE SELDON for a brief moment, then looks across to the desk and filing cabinet in the far corner of the room. He gives a look of surprise and moves quickly to the desk. The drawers of both the desk and filing cabinet are open. Papers are strewn on the top of the desk and an envelope containing papers is lying on the floor nearby. Someone has made a hurried search of the drawers. LARRY picks up the envelope and the fallen papers and puts them on the desk. He glances at the filing cabinet and turns away. A file is balanced precariously on one of the open drawers. LARRY takes hold of the file with the intention of replacing it in the drawer. As he does so, something flutters to the floor. LARRY stares down at his feet. He sinks down to a crouching position to pick up one of the fallen articles. We see it in his hand. It is a photograph. It is apparently a copy of the

58

photograph of SEAN REYNOLDS and his wife. LARRY stares at the photograph for a moment or two, then looks down at his feet. There are two or three more copies of the same photograph on the floor. LARRY picks up the photographs and opens the file to return them. The file contains more copies of apparently the same photograph. LARRY looks hastily through them. There are about a dozen altogether. Puzzled, LARRY puts the photographs inside the files and places it in the drawer. He stands there for a moment. He remembers THOMAS QUAYLE and moves to the door leading up to the interior of the shop. He calls up the stairs.

LARRY: (*Calling*) Mr Quayle?

Silence.

LARRY: Mr Quayle?

LARRY listens. Suddenly there is the sound of a car starting in the street above, immediately outside the house. LARRY turns back into the room, crossing to the small window. There is the sound of a car driving away. LARRY moves quickly to the door leading to the street stairs.

CUT TO: The exterior of QUAYLE's antique shop.

LARRY runs up the stairs to the pavement. He stands there looking up and down the street. He is bewildered. The street is empty, except for a WOMAN wheeling a pram yards further along. LARRY turns to look once again in the other direction. He takes a cigarette from his pocket (the one he took out earlier and didn't light) and puts it in his mouth. He turns and looks in the direction of his car. He takes out his lighter and lights his cigarette. As he returns the lighter to his pocket he suddenly freezes, staring ahead. He moves slowly forward, his eyes fixed on something ahead of him. We now see what it is that has attracted LARRY's attention. It is an object hanging from the closed boot; THOMAS QUAYLE's watch – the chain caught in the closing of the boot. LARRY moves suddenly

*forward, turns the handle, and wrenches open the boot.
THOMAS QUAYLE's body is in it. There is a knife in his
chest.*

END OF EPISODE TWO

EPISODE THREE

OPEN TO: The exterior of THOMAS QUAYLE's shop.

An object is hanging from the closed boot; THOMAS QUAYLE's watch – the chain caught in the closing of the boot. LARRY moves suddenly forward, turns the handle, and wrenches open the boot. THOMAS QUAYLE's body is in it. There is a knife in his chest. LARRY stares at the body and then makes a sudden move forward. Instinctively LARRY touches QUAYLE's motionless body. With a sudden movement he withdraws his hand and slams down the cover of the boot. He looks quickly up and down the street, makes a decision, and moves briskly to the door of the antique shop and goes in.

CUT TO: The interior of QUAYLE's antique shop. *LARRY quickly enters and goes to the telephone with the bookrest containing the book of poems by Hilaire Belloc just behind it. LARRY lifts the receiver and dials 999. He is tense and worried.*

CUT TO: The London-Arundel Road.

A police car is parked at the roadside facing a sign which reads – Arundel Welcomes Careful Drivers.

Two uniformed policemen stand near the car. One of them has seen a car approaching from the direction of London and bends to the window of the police car to inform the occupant, who nods and gets out of the car. He is DETECTIVE INSPECTOR LANG. A second police car draws up and INSPECTOR HYDE gets out. LANG hurries to him and they shake hands and after exchanging brief greetings, move briskly to LANG's car. They get in, followed by the uniformed men, and the car moves off in the direction of Arundel.

CUT TO: The interior of the police car.

LANG and HYDE are sitting side by side discussing the death of THOMAS QUAYLE.

LANG: … Quayle was dead when we got there. There was a knife in his chest and I should say he'd been dead about ten minutes.

HYDE: What did Martin say?

LANG: He was helpful but he refused to make a statement. When we got back to the Station we took his fingerprints and I think that put the wind up him. He said he wanted to see you – that's why I phoned.

HYDE: Tell me a little more about Mr Quayle.

LANG: I'm afraid I don't know a great deal about him. He was a bachelor; seemed to be pretty well off. He has a sister. She runs a hotel in Maidenhead.

HYDE: Maidenhead?

LANG: Yes.

HYDE: Her name isn't Curtis, by any chance?

LANG: Yes, that's right – Mrs Curtis. The Royal Falcon. (*Curious*) Why – do you know her?

HYDE: Yes, I do. Martin's brother died, under rather unusual circumstances, at the Royal Falcon.

LANG: Did he? When was this?

HYDE: About a week ago.

LANG: Now that's interesting …

HYDE: Have you sent for Mrs Curtis?

LANG: Yes, she's down here – arrived about an hour ago.

HYDE: How did she take it?

LANG: It's difficult to say; she was upset, of course. She came down with a chap called Douglas Talbot.

HYDE: Yes, he runs the hotel for her.

LANG: Pompous ass; never stops asking questions. I think he considers himself a bit of a Private-Eye.

HYDE smiles.

LANG: Why do you think Larry Martin saw Quayle – was it to question him about his brother?

HYDE: I think so. Martin's convinced it wasn't suicide. He thinks his brother was murdered.

LANG: And what do you think?

HYDE: We've got no proof that it was murder, so obviously I …

LANG: (*Smiling; interrupting him*) That's not what I asked you.

HYDE looks at Lang and hesitates for a moment.

HYDE: Frankly, I'm inclined to agree with Martin. There's something funny about this business – damn funny. I suppose you read about the Knightsbridge shooting – young service chap called Andy Wilson?

LANG: Yes.

HYDE: Well, he was a friend of Philip Martin's. He'd just left Larry's studio when some character in a car took a pot shot at him. He was damn lucky he wasn't killed.

LANG: Have you seen Wilson?

HYDE: Yes, I saw him this morning. I tried to talk to him about a photograph, but I couldn't get anything out of him.

LANG: A photograph?

HYDE: Yes.

LANG: I suppose it wasn't a photograph of a man and a woman – the woman playing an accordion?

HYDE: (*Surprised*) Yes, it was.

LANG: Well, that's very odd, to say the least. Martin made us collect a book and some photographs from Quayle's antique shop. He said you'd be interested in them.

65

HYDE:	(*Quickly*) What was the book?
LANG:	It was a book of poems by – now what the devil's the chap's name?
HYDE:	Belloc? Hilaire Belloc?
LANG:	Yes, that's right! That's the fellow …
HYDE:	Then Mr Martin's right. (*Thoughtfully*) I am interested …

CUT TO: A Street in Arundel.
A police car proceeds along the street.

CUT TO: An office in Arundel Police Station.
A uniformed sergeant is seated near the corner of a desk taking notes. There is a cup of tea on the desk and the book of poems from Quayle's antique shop. HYDE picks up the cup. LARRY is seated on the other side of the desk.

LARRY:	… So I arranged to meet Mrs Curtis at the café.
HYDE:	(*Picking up a key from the desk*) Taking this key with you?
LARRY:	Yes.
HYDE:	And when she refused to talk you decided to come down here and see Quayle?
LARRY:	Yes.
HYDE:	(*With the suggestion of a smile*) In other words, you'd made up your mind to swap the key for – information?
LARRY:	Yes, you can put it that way, if you like.
HYDE:	You must have thought this key was pretty important, Mr Martin?
LARRY:	I got the impression it was important.
HYDE:	From Mrs Curtis?
LARRY:	From both Mrs Curtis and Quayle.
HYDE:	Now tell me again what happened when this woman – Mrs Seldon – returned to the shop.

LARRY: I was talking to Quayle; I'd just told him about the attempt on his sister's life. He was rather shaken, he obviously knew nothing about it. I then asked him whether he thought Phil had committed suicide and he said No – he'd been murdered. At that moment Mrs Seldon came back into the shop.

HYDE: Go on, Mr Martin …

LARRY: She told Quayle she wanted to take another look at a nest of tables. They went down into the basement. After about two or three minutes, Mrs Seldon returned, alone. I heard Quayle's voice from the basement, but I didn't see him. After Mrs Seldon had gone, I strolled about the shop, waiting for Quayle to return. It was then that I saw the book.

HYDE: (*Nodding*) This Mrs Seldon – I take it you'd recognise her again?

LARRY: Yes, I would.

HYDE: Do you think she had anything to do with this business?

LARRY: (*After a moment*) Yes, I do. It's my bet the people who murdered Quayle turned up while I was talking to him. They entered the basement while she came back into the shop and talked Quayle into showing her the nest of tables.

HYDE: And when Quayle went downstairs her friends were waiting for him?

LARRY: Yes.

HYDE: But I thought you said you heard his voice when Mrs Seldon was leaving?

LARRY: I did.

HYDE: Well, how do you account for that?

LARRY: Someone could have been telling him what to say – someone with a knife, for instance.

HYDE looks at LARRY for a moment and then picks up one of the photographs; he compares it with the others on the desk.

LARRY: They're all the same; they're reproductions of the one that Phil showed me; the one that was in the showcase.

HYDE: (*Noncommittal*) Yes.

LARRY: Incidentally, the last time we met you said that you were going to see Andy Wilson.

HYDE: I've seen him.

LARRY: Did you ask him what he meant by that remark – about the photograph?

HYDE: Yes, I asked him; but he didn't tell me.

LARRY: Why? Was he too ill to talk, or …

HYDE: No, he was all right. He just wouldn't talk, that's all.

LARRY: Do you think he'd talk to me?

HYDE looks up; he gives the matter thought.

HYDE: I don't know, Mr Martin. He might.

HYDE looks at the photographs again, studying each one separately. LARRY watches him.

HYDE: (*Casually; not looking up*) Did you touch the knife?

LARRY: (*Surprised by the question*) The knife?

HYDE: Yes – the one that killed him.

LARRY: (*Faintly bewildered*) I don't know. I can't remember. I might have done … Why?

HYDE: (*With almost a shrug; casually*) They found your fingerprints on it.

HYDE picks up another photograph and examines it. He ignores LARRY.

CUT TO: As before. The office at Arundel Police Station. *VANESSA CURTIS and DOUGLAS TALBOT are being questioned by HYDE and INSPECTOR LANG. HYDE is sitting on the chair previously occupied by the sergeant. INSPECTOR LANG is at the desk; he is faintly irritated by TALBOT.*

TALBOT: ... I'm sure Mrs Curtis would like to get back to Maidenhead as soon as possible, so if there are any other questions, Inspector ...

LANG: (*Interrupting him*) If you'll just bear with us a moment or two longer, sir. Now, Mrs Curtis – you say that you've never heard of Mrs Seldon and you don't know why your brother had these photographs or the book? (*He indicates the photographs and book on the desk*)

VANESSA: No. The photographs are a complete mystery, I've never seen them before. The book ... (*A shrug*) ... My brother was an intellectual. He read all kinds of books.

HYDE: Yes, but it's the same book that Philip Martin was reading, a book of poems, Mrs Curtis. Doesn't it strike you as being a rather strange coincidence that your brother should have displayed a copy of the same book in his antique shop?

TALBOT: Look, Inspector – hasn't it occurred to you that perhaps Thomas knew nothing about the book or the photographs?

HYDE: No, sir – that hasn't occurred to me.

TALBOT: You were told about the book and the photographs by Mr Martin after Thomas had been murdered.

HYDE: Yes.

TALBOT: Then isn't it possible that Martin's lying and he brought both the book and the photographs down here, himself?

69

HYDE: Yes, it's possible. But why should Martin do
             that?

TALBOT: I don't know why, but Mr Martin seems to be
             doing quite a lot of peculiar things just lately.

LANG: What are you referring to, sir?

TALBOT hesitates; looks at VANESSA.

VANESSA: Douglas – Mr Talbot – has a theory. He
             doesn't believe that Larry Martin's been
             telling the truth about his brother.

HYDE: Oh? This is interesting. Why don't you think
             he's telling the truth, sir?

TALBOT: Well – Martin said that he was surprised
             when he found out his brother was staying at
             the Falcon …

HYDE nods.

TALBOT: … he was under the impression that he was in
             Ireland.

HYDE: Yes.

TALBOT: I don't believe that! I believe that Larry
             Martin knew all the time his brother was at
             Maidenhead. I think Mr Martin is trying to
             bamboozle everybody. It's my opinion he
             knows perfectly well what Philip Martin was
             doing at the Falcon.

HYDE: What was he doing?

TALBOT: I don't know, I wish I did.

HYDE: Then all this is just supposition?

TALBOT: Supposition based on fact.

HYDE: What fact?

TALBOT: The fact that, by a strange coincidence, Larry
             Martin happened to be friendly with someone
             at the hotel.

HYDE: (*Interested*) Oh? Who was that?

TALBOT: A Dr Linderhof.

HYDE: He was the German – from Hamburg?

TALBOT: That's right.

HYDE: (*Intrigued*) Now let's get this straight. You say that Larry Martin knew Dr Linderhof?

TALBOT: (*With a faintly satisfied smile*) Yes, that's the point I'm trying to convey, Inspector.

HYDE: How do you know this?

TALBOT: Shortly after Philip Martin committed suicide Dr Linderhof made a phone call. I accidentally overheard part of it. I didn't know who he was speaking to, but the name Philip was mentioned several times. Naturally, I was curious.

HYDE: Go on …

TALBOT: Linderhof made an appointment to see the person he was talking to. When he'd finished the call, I checked with the switchboard and got the number.

HYDE: It was Larry Martin's?

TALBOT: Yes.

HYDE: Why haven't you told me about this phone call before?

TALBOT: I wasn't so sure that it was important. (*He looks at LANG*) In any case, it's not very easy to tell the police anything. They seem to know the lot.

HYDE: (*Annoyed*) Not quite the lot, sir.

CUT TO: LARRY MARTIN's Studio.

This room adjoins the living room of LARRY's flat. It is the following morning.

RUTH is seated on a bar stool by a bar on the beach in the South of France – at least, that is what the set-up makes it look like. LARRY is checking some lighting for a photo shoot.

LARRY: Look up again …

71

RUTH looks up, effecting a smile. LARRY looks at her critically for a moment, then moves to another lamp, adjusting it.

LARRY: That's it. Thanks.

Ruth rises and joins LARRY.

LARRY: Well, that'll save moans from Carol about waiting around for me to set up. She's always in a frantic hurry these days.

RUTH: I don't know what she has to moan about. You'd think she was the only model in London who could wear a swimsuit.

The doorbell rings.

LARRY: There she is, Ruth. Don't keep the young lady waiting.

RUTH gives him a look and goes out through the door to the living room. LARRY smiles to himself and then towards the Riviera set-up. He studies it for a moment and then moves to adjust the bar stool when he hears HYDE's voice as he comes through from the living room.

HYDE's VOICE: I hope he's not in the middle of a session?

LARRY looks up and turns towards the door. RUTH returns.

RUTH: No – he's just about to begin one.

HYDE follows RUTH into the studio.

RUTH: Inspector Hyde …

LARRY: Oh – good morning, Inspector.

HYDE: Good morning, Mr Martin.

HYDE's manner is a little distant, less friendly than it was the previous afternoon at Arundel. RUTH turns, to return to the living room, but HYDE stops her.

HYDE: Don't go, Miss Sanders, I want to have a word with you if Mr Martin has no objection.

LARRY looks at RUTH as she hesitates, obviously surprised by HYDE's remark.

LARRY: If you've got anything to ask my secretary – go ahead.

HYDE: (*To LARRY*) You told me that Mr Quayle called here and asked you for the key – the one the porter gave you by mistake.

LARRY: Yes, that's right.

HYDE: (*Suddenly; to RUTH*) Did you see Mr Quayle, Miss Sanders?

RUTH: Yes, I did. I showed him into the flat.

HYDE: What was he wearing?

RUTH: (*After a moment*) He had a dark overcoat with a velvet collar – and a bowler hat. He also had a little dog with him. He called it Whitie – a sweet little thing …

HYDE nods, dismissing RUTH.

HYDE: Thank you, Miss Sanders.

RUTH looks to LARRY and then goes out into the living room.

LARRY: (*Irritated*) I hope you're satisfied, Inspector.

HYDE: Yes, sir. I'm satisfied. (*Looking at the Riviera set-up*) Mr Martin, d'you know a man called Harris – Luther Harris?

LARRY: Yes.

HYDE: What do you know about him?

LARRY: He was a friend of my brother's. He has a music shop on the Tottenham Court Road. "Pop's Corner", I think they call it.

HYDE: Yes, that's right, sir. Is he a friend of Andy Wilson's?

LARRY: Yes. Phil and Andy always made a point of dropping in on him when they were on leave. They used to spend hours listening to his gramophone records. (*A faint smile*) Although I don't think they ever bought one.

HYDE: Have you met Mr Harris?

LARRY: Yes.

HYDE: When?

LARRY: Oh, I've bumped into him on several occasions
          when I've been out with my brother. But why are
          you interested in Harris?

HYDE: He paid Andy Wilson a visit yesterday morning.

LARRY: That doesn't surprise me; he's a friend of Andy's.
          He wrote me a very nice letter when – my brother
          died.

*HYDE nods; he looks about him, curiously interested in the
studio.*

LARRY: How is Andy?

HYDE: (*Turning*) He's going to get better, Mr Martin.
          But he still refuses to talk – he won't say anything
          about the book or the photograph. Incidentally, he
          wants to see you. I've told him you'll drop in this
          evening.

*LARRY nods. HYDE takes a photograph from his inside
pocket.*

HYDE: This is one of the photographs you found at
          Quayle's. I want you to take another look at it.

LARRY: Why?

HYDE: I'd just like you to take another look at it, sir.

*We see the photograph we've seen before – a man and a
woman; the man standing behind the woman who is sitting
and playing an accordion.*

LARRY: Well?

HYDE indicates the photograph in LARRY's hand.

HYDE: You don't know those people? You haven't the
          slightest idea who they are? (*Quietly; watching
          him*) Is that right, sir?

LARRY: (*Irritated*) Yes, of course it's right! Of course, I
          don't know them! I've told you this before …

74

HYDE looks at LARRY for a second and then takes the photograph from him.

HYDE: Yes, you have, Mr Martin. Thank you. (*He puts the photograph in his pocket*)

LARRY: (*Faintly "on edge"*) Now, is there anything else, Inspector, because I've got a very busy morning and I don't want to waste …

HYDE: (*Interrupting him*) Yes, there is something else, sir. You've told me – (*A faint smile*) on several occasions – that you haven't the slightest idea what your brother was doing at Maidenhead.

LARRY: That's true – I haven't …

HYDE: But surely there could be a very simple explanation, sir. It must have occurred to you.

LARRY: What do you mean?

HYDE: Isn't it possible your brother went down to Maidenhead to see a friend of yours?

LARRY: A friend of mine?

HYDE: Yes; Dr Linderhof.

LARRY stares at HYDE in astonishment.

LARRY: Who told you Dr Linderhof was a friend of mine?

HYDE: (*With a touch of authority*) Is he a friend of yours, sir?

LARRY: No, most certainly not! Why – why, I've only met the man once.

HYDE: And when was that, Mr Martin?

LARRY: Two days ago.

HYDE: And where did you meet him?

LARRY: Here – he came to the flat.

HYDE looks at LARRY; he sits on the arm of a chair.

HYDE: Don't you think it would be a good idea if you told me about Dr Linderhof, sir?

LARRY: (*A moment; faintly perturbed*) Yes, I do. I intended to tell you next week, Inspector, but …

75

HYDE: Tell me now, sir.

LARRY: I went down to Maidenhead to see Mrs Curtis. When I got back Dr Linderhof was here – waiting for me.

HYDE: Were you expecting him?

LARRY: No, of course not, I'd never met the man. He told me that he'd overheard a conversation between Mrs Curtis and my brother and that under the circumstances I ought to know about it.

HYDE: How did he overhear this conversation?

LARRY: He was taken ill and went to the bathroom. It was next to my brother's room.

HYDE: And when did this happen, exactly?

LARRY: It was about half past one in the morning – eight hours before they found Phil.

HYDE: (*Quietly*) Go on …

LARRY: Dr Linderhof said he heard my brother say, "I'm going back to London, whatever happens. I'm not spending another minute reading that book and waiting for that friend of yours." … Mrs Curtis replied, "You've got to wait until he arrives, Phil – even if it means another week, you've got to wait."

HYDE: Did Linderhof hear anything else?

LARRY: Yes, he heard Phil say, "I'm not waiting a day longer and that's final …"

HYDE: And that's all he heard?

LARRY: Yes.

HYDE: (*Rising*) Well, it's an interesting story – but why didn't Dr Linderhof tell it to me instead of to you, Mr Martin?

LARRY: He's apparently in trouble. He comes up before the German medical authorities one day next week and he doesn't want any publicity. He was frightened that if he got in touch with the police …

76

HYDE: (*Interrupting him*) I get the point, Mr Martin.

The door opens and RUTH enters with CAROL LANE. RUTH carries a notebook and pencil. CAROL is a professional model; a jet-propelled blonde.

HYDE: I'll leave you to get on with your work, sir. Give me a ring when you see Andy Wilson; I'd like to know what happens. If I'm not at the Yard you can get me at Kensington 7876.

RUTH makes a note of the number. HYDE gives CAROL a quick glance and goes out. RUTH looks at LARRY, curious to know what has happened, then she follows the INSPECTOR into the living room.

CAROL: (*To LARRY*) I hope this isn't going to take long, sweetie. I'm in a frantic hurry – I've got to be at the Savoy at twelve o'clock.

CAROL quickly takes off her dress, revealing the fact that she is already wearing a swimsuit underneath. She takes her position on the bar stool. LARRY is deep in thought, completely unaware of CAROL's presence.

CUT TO: A Hospital Ward.

ANDY WILSON is lying in the end bed with the wall of the ward running alongside it. He is propped up with several pillows, reading a newspaper. He turns slightly on hearing someone approaching. A fleeting look of apprehension crosses his face, and he looks back at the newspaper. A NURSE arrives placing a chair at the bedside.

NURSE: A visitor for you, Mr Wilson.

LARRY appears behind the NURSE. ANDY lowers the paper and looks up as the NURSE turns to LARRY.

NURSE: Only a few minutes, I'm afraid, Mr Martin.

LARRY: (*Nodding*) Thank you.

The NURSE goes. ANDY looks straight ahead as LARRY comes to the bed.

LARRY: Well, Andy – how are you feeling now?

ANDY still doesn't look at him.

ANDY: Oh – can't grumble, I suppose.

LARRY glances down at the chair; decides to sit. There is an awkward pause)

LARRY: Well – here I am. You did say you wanted to see me?

ANDY: (*Grudgingly*) Yes, I did.

LARRY: (*After a moment*) Have you got everything you want here? I mean – well – if there's anything you need …

ANDY: (*Curtly*) I'm all right, thanks.

LARRY: (*Quietly*) You've got something to tell me, haven't you, Andy?

ANDY turns slightly away.

ANDY: Yes. (*A moment*) I'm – I'm sorry about the book, Larry. I shouldn't have taken it.

LARRY: Why did you take it?

ANDY: I don't know.

LARRY: Now, Andy, please – don't insult my intelligence. You wanted that book for a particular reason …

ANDY: Yes …

LARRY: What was the reason?

ANDY doesn't answer.

LARRY: All right, if you won't tell me about the book – tell me about Phil. What was he doing at Maidenhead?

ANDY still doesn't answer.

LARRY: What was Phil mixed up in? I've got a right to know, Andy. I'm his brother.

ANDY looks at him for a moment, then looks away. He is obviously not going to give LARRY the answer to this.

LARRY: Look, if you don't intend to talk, why did you send for me?

ANDY: I – I wanted to warn you.

LARRY: Warn me?

ANDY: Yes.

LARRY: About what?

ANDY: You know what happened to Phil. It wasn't suicide – he was murdered.

LARRY: (*Nodding*) Yes, I know that.

ANDY: Well – I don't want the same thing to happen to you; and it will happen to you, Larry, unless …

LARRY: Unless what?

ANDY: Unless you stop interfering.

LARRY: (*Quietly*) What would you suggest? That I go home and forget the whole business? That I stop trying to find out why my brother was murdered?

ANDY: (*Tensely*) Yes …

LARRY looks at Andy; shakes his head.

LARRY: You're scared – you're really scared, aren't you, Andy?

ANDY: Yes, I'm scared – I'm scared to hell and I don't care who knows it! These people are desperate, Larry – once they make up their mind to … (*He stops; frightened*)

LARRY: Go on …

ANDY gives LARRY a quick look and then turns away from him.

LARRY: (*Quietly*) Go on, Andy … Who are these people?

ANDY: (*Softly; distressed*) I don't know … I've said too much already … I … Larry, I'm sorry, I don't feel too good – please leave me alone …

LARRY: (*Quietly; leaning towards the bed*) Andy, listen – you may as well understand this right now. I'm going through with this. I'm not giving up until I find out what it was Phil was mixed up in and why he was murdered.

ANDY: All right – if that's the way you want it, go ahead. But I've warned you, Larry – I've told you what'll happen …

LARRY rises; looks down at ANDY.

LARRY: What was Phil mixed up in? Who are these people?

ANDY: I'm sorry, Larry – I've said too much already … (*Shaking his head*) I'm not saying anything else. (*He lifts himself up slightly from the bed and raises his voice*) Nurse!

LARRY stands looking down at ANDY; tense and serious. After a moment the NURSE appears.

NURSE: Did you call, Mr Wilson?

ANDY: Yes, I'm afraid I'm too tired to talk – I want to go to sleep, Nurse.

The NURSE is faintly surprised. She looks at LARRY.

NURSE: I'm sorry, Mr Martin.

LARRY: (*Nodding*) That's all right. (*He looks at ANDY*) Goodbye, Andy.

LARRY hesitates, then goes. After a moment ANDY turns and looks in the direction of the door. His expression is one of anger and self-reproach.

CUT TO: Outside LARRY MARTIN's flat.
LARRY's car drives into the mews and stops outside the entrance to his flat. LARRY gets out and goes through the entrance to the stairs.

CUT TO: The front door of LARRY MARTIN's flat.
LARRY crosses from the stairs to his front door, feeling in his pocket for his door key. He takes out the key and tries to insert it in the lock when he hesitates. He listens. Imagining he has heard a sound from within the flat. He looks at the key,

then very carefully inserts it in the lock and slowly, gently opens the door.

CUT TO: The living room of LARRY MARTIN's flat.
The sole lighting comes from the lamp on the desk. The drawers of the desk are open, and a woman's gloved hands are searching through them. LARRY comes into the doorway and stares at the direction of the intruder, who has her back to him. LARRY remains there for a moment, watching, before he speaks.

LARRY: Can I help you?

The woman swings around to stare at LARRY. She is startled, frightened by his sudden appearance. We now see that she is the woman who bought the lamp at Quayle's antique shop – CLARE SELDON. She doesn't speak. LARRY moves slowly toward her. CLARE's eyes flicker towards the partly open door to the studio. LARRY sees the look.

LARRY: I'm afraid you can't get out that way.

CLARE: (*Calling out*) Fletcher!

LARRY looks in the direction of the studio door. He makes to go into the studio, stops, realising that perhaps CLARE is trying to trick him in order to make her getaway. He remains there indecisively for a moment.

LARRY: Look – what are you searching for?

He stops as a man appears in the studio doorway; a dark, saturnine looking man, about thirty. He wears a belted raincoat, no hat. This is CLIFF FLETCHER. FLETCHER remains in the doorway, watching LARRY with narrowed eyes, obviously waiting for LARRY to make a false move. LARRY steps towards him. FLETCHER puts his hand inside the lapel of his raincoat. LARRY hesitates. FLETCHER keeps his hand inside his raincoat.

LARRY: Who the hell are you? And what are you doing here?

FLETCHER looks across at CLARE, nodding towards the hall door. LARRY looks at CLARE. CLARE, with obvious relief, hurries out. There is a moment's silence. The front door slams shut as CLARE leaves the flat. LARRY looks at FLETCHER.

LARRY: What is it you want? What are you supposed to be looking for?

FLETCHER: The key, Mr Martin.

LARRY: The key? You mean the one that Mrs Curtis …

FLETCHER: You know the key I mean …

LARRY hesitates, his eyes lowered to FLETCHER's hand inside the raincoat.

FLETCHER: Well? Do I get it?

There is a movement under the raincoat, the hand obviously tightening around the handle of a weapon.

LARRY: No, I'm afraid you don't. I gave it to the Inspector.

FLETCHER, with the faintest of smiles, moves towards LARRY.

FLETCHER: Oh yes – you gave the original key to the Inspector, I know that …

LARRY: What do you mean – the original key?

FLETCHER: When you left the café you took the key to an ironmonger's and had a duplicate made. I know what I'm talking about, Martin, so don't let's waste time – hand it over.

There is only about eighteen inches between them now. LARRY looks down once more at the hand beneath the raincoat and suddenly he nods, and keeping a watchful eye on FLETCHER, moves to the desk. He stops near the telephone, which is next to an open box-type file, opened during the search of his desk. He looks at FLETCHER then turns away – as he does so he makes a sudden movement towards the telephone, as if reaching to lift the receiver. FLETCHER

82

whips out a knife from inside his raincoat. With a vicious expression he hurls the knife at LARRY. We hear the knife thud into its target but then we see that LARRY is holding the box-file at chest level; the knife is embedded in it. FLETCHER swears and runs to the door. LARRY hurls aside the box-file and rushes after him. LARRY reaches FLETCHER in the doorway, hauling him back into the room by the belt of his raincoat. LARRY makes to punch him, but FLETCHER kicks out, catching LARRY in the side. LARRY manages to grasp FLETCHER's leg and he topples to the ground, his leg still held. As FLETCHER kicks and struggles to free himself his wallet slides out of his pocket, unnoticed by both of them. It falls to the floor, and FLETCHER, in his struggles, pushes it under a corner of the desk. With a final vicious wrench FLETCHER frees his leg and jumps to his feet as LARRY moves to him. In almost the same moment he pulls out one of the open drawers from the desk and swings around with it. The drawer splinters and LARRY falls to the floor on his knees. FLETCHER runs out of the flat. LARRY, dazed by the blow, suddenly rises to his feet, his hands nursing one side of his head. We now see the wallet under the corner of the desk, not far from LARRY's feet. LARRY staggers to the settee and collapses onto it. He shakes his head and looks dazedly in the direction of the door, now becoming aware that FLETCHER has gone. He rises to his feet and moves unsteadily towards the door. The telephone rings. LARRY stops in the doorway, turning to look at it. He moves to the desk, one hand still nursing his cheek, and picks up the receiver.

LARRY: Yes?

RUTH's VOICE: Larry? …

LARRY: Oh … Ruth … It's you …

RUTH's VOICE: Larry – I forgot to tell you before I left today, Parker and Anderson rang about those prints for the dental cream …

LARRY: It can wait, Ruth. Tell me tomorrow!

RUTH's VOICE: Larry, are you all right? …

LARRY: Yes … I've had a bit of a crack on the head and I … I'm sorry, Ruth – I can't talk now …

LARRY replaces the receiver. He stands by the desk for a moment, then crosses to the settee. He sits and leans back, nursing the side of his head in his hands.

CUT TO: The living room of LARRY MARTIN's flat.
About an hour later.

RUTH is at the drinks table, pouring a whisky. Her coat is draped over a nearby chair. She takes the whisky across to LARRY, who is seated on the settee, a sticking-plaster on the cut above his left eye.

LARRY: Thanks.

LARRY takes the drink and sips it. RUTH takes up the first-aid kit on the settee alongside LARRY and puts away the nail scissors and sticking-plaster during the following conversation.

RUTH: This woman – what was her name?

LARRY: Seldon – Mrs Seldon.

RUTH: Are you sure it was the woman you saw in Arundel – the one in the antique shop?

LARRY: Positive. She was there when I arrived – buying some furniture. She couldn't make up her mind about a nest of tables. She came back later and Quayle took her down to the basement.

RUTH: What about the man?

LARRY: I've never seen him before. (*Feeling his head*) I'm not so sure I want to see him again.

84

RUTH: The thing I don't understand is – how did he know
          about the key – the duplicate one?

LARRY: Someone must have followed me when I left the
          café.

RUTH: (*Nodding*) Yes, I suppose so. (*Curious*) Larry,
          why did you have the key copied?

LARRY: Both Mrs Curtis and Quayle obviously attached
          importance to it, so I thought the best thing I could
          do … (*He stops speaking; obviously having
          noticed something under the desk*) Ruth, what's
          that – under the desk?

*RUTH looks at the corner of the desk; crosses to it and picks
up FLETCHER's wallet.*

LARRY: He must have dropped it …

RUTH: Yes.

*LARRY takes the wallet and slowly examines it. There are the
initials on the wallet – C.F.*

LARRY: C.F. … Yes, she shouted "Fletcher" …

*He opens the wallet and takes out three five-pound notes and
a square card; a dance ticket. LARRY looks at the card.*

RUTH: What is it?

LARRY: It's a dance ticket. (*Looking at the ticket*) Imperial
          Hotel, Camden Town … September the 29th …
          (*He looks at RUTH*) I wonder if that's the dance
          Phil was going to?

RUTH: Was he going to a dance?

RUTH takes the ticket from LARRY and looks at it.

LARRY: Yes – he mentioned it, that first morning. He told
          me not to make arrangements for … What are you
          looking at, Ruth?

Ruth has turned the card over and is examining the back of it.

RUTH: Somebody's written three names on the back of
          the card – look, Larry …

LARRY takes the card from RUTH and looks at it. We see three names – PHILIP MARTIN, ANDY WILSON, LUTHER HARRIS – have been written on the back of the ticket.

RUTH: Who's Luther Harris?

LARRY: (*Thoughtfully*) He was a friend of Phil's. He has a
          music shop on Tottenham Court Road.

RUTH: (*Remembering*) Oh yes – that's right, I remember
          Phil talking about him …

LARRY looks at the ticket again.

RUTH: September the 29th … That's tomorrow.

LARRY: Yes. (*He looks up at Ruth; hesitates*) Are you a
          good dancer, Ruth?

RUTH: There's only one way to find out.

(*LARRY smiles at her*)

CUT TO: Outside the Imperial Hotel; a large, depressed looking building.

LARRY's car draws up at the kerb and LARRY gets out. He goes around the car and helps RUTH out of the passenger seat. She is <u>NOT</u> carrying her handbag. They cross to the hotel entrance where people are arriving for the dance.

CUT TO: The Foyer of the Imperial Hotel.

A large display card on an easel near the entrance from the street reads – "Grand Dance – in aid of the United Services Hostel – tonight from 8.30 till midnight – tickets   12/6d." Near the display card stands a dark, moustached man with patent leather shoes and hair to match – a kind of cherry blossomed Fred Astaire; obviously the local cha-cha champion, or something equally illustrious, as people appear to recognise him as they jostle through the entrance and move towards the dance hall.

LARRY and RUTH come through the entrance and stand just inside, taking in the scene. The cha-cha champion eyes RUTH

86

up and down. From inside the dance hall come the strains of the band fiendishly shredding and blasting an old favourite. LARRY steers RUTH away from the jostling doorway.

RUTH: (*Quietly*) I've decided to tell the truth.

LARRY looks at her a little vaguely.

RUTH: I can't dance a step.

LARRY: (*Smiling*) Well – now's your chance to learn. *Before RUTH can retort LARRY steers her in the direction of a trestle table where a man is selling tickets. Behind the trestle is a large hand-painted poster advertising the band. It reads – "Monty Fry and the Frymen – Frying Tonight – featuring Joe Glazer on trumpet and Gerry Waller on drums". Underneath this is a picture of a blonde singer, her lungs well displayed. RUTH stares at this poster and the photograph while LARRY buys the tickets.*

LARRY: Two, please.

TICKET MAN: Thank you, sir.

LARRY gives the man two one-pound notes and while he is waiting for his change, he glances across at a rather flashily dressed GIRL in her mid-twenties, who is looking impatiently in the direction of the cloakroom. At the cloakroom a crowd of jostling men are endeavouring to hand their coats over the counter. LARRY starts to unbutton his overcoat as he glances around the foyer.

LARRY: (*To RUTH*) Well – I'd better join in the Battle of the Overcoats. Oh – there's your place over there, look. I'll see you back here … (*He stops, staring in the direction of the cloakroom*)

The flashily dressed girl is looking in the same direction. She gives a short, sharp sign as she sees someone emerging from the crowd at the counter. The man leaving the counter is LUTHER HARRIS, a shrewd, porky little man with rimless glasses; he is in his early forties. He moves to his girlfriend, intent on putting his cloakroom ticket into his pocket. As he looks up he sees LARRY staring at him. He appears not to recognise LARRY, looks away with a quick, nervous smile at his girlfriend, and crosses quickly to her, taking her arm.

LUTHER: Sorry, Peg …

PEGGY: Thought you was never comin' …

LUTHER quickly steers her towards the dance hall entrance.

LARRY: (*Calling*) Luther!

LUTHER pauses for a brief moment before turning.

LUTHER: Well – hello, Larry! Fancy seeing you here! Never expected to find you in this sort of place …

LARRY: (*Smiling*) No, I'm afraid this was Ruth's idea – she's fond of dancing … (*To RUTH*) Oh, sorry, Ruth … Mr Harris … Miss Sanders …

LUTHER: (*Nodding*) How do you do?

LARRY: (*To RUTH*) Luther was a friend of Phil's.

RUTH: Oh, yes, of course. (*Smiling at LUTHER*) I remember now …

LUTHER: (*Indicating his girlfriend*) This is my fiancée – Peggy Grahame.

LARRY: (*To Peggy*) Hello? …

PEGGY: Delighted, I'm sure …

LUTHER: How have you been keeping, Larry?

LARRY: Oh, I've been all right – considering.

LUTHER: It was terrible about Phil. I was awfully upset when I heard about it …

LARRY: Yes, I know. Thank you for your letter, Luther. I didn't reply because …

LUTHER: (*With a gesture*) No, of course not … (*A pause*) Well – we'll be seeing you …

LARRY: Yes, perhaps we could join up later. I'd like to have a talk with you, Luther.

LUTHER: (*Looking at LARRY*) Yes ... yes, of course.

RUTH: (*To Peggy*) Is there a bar here?

88

PEGGY: My God, I hope so!

LUTHER: It's up on the first floor. We could meet up there if you like.

LARRY: Yes, that's a good idea – let's do that. Say about ten o'clock?

LUTHER: Fine. (*He looks at RUTH*) See you later, then.

He nods to LARRY and takes PEGGY's arm. She gives another forced smile and goes off with LUTHER into the dance hall. LARRY watches them go.

RUTH: He's a strange little man.

LARRY: Yes.

RUTH: How well did he know Phil?

LARRY: I'm not sure. I think they saw quite a bit of each other.

RUTH: I don't think he really wanted to talk to you, Larry.

LARRY: No; that was my impression.

RUTH: Well, I suppose we'd better go in … Oh dear!

LARRY: What's the matter?

RUTH: I've left my handbag in the car.

LARRY: I'll fetch it for you.

RUTH: No, please – I'll get it if you'll give me the key.

LARRY takes out his keys, selects the car key, and hands them to her.

RUTH: Thanks.

RUTH goes. LARRY crosses to the cloakroom. He folds his overcoat and hands it to the man behind the counter.

ATTENDANT: Sixpence, please, sir …

LARRY feels in his trouser pocket as the ATTENDANT pins a ticket on LARRY's overcoat. RUTH comes in at the entrance from the street. She is still without her handbag and looks very excited. She looks across at LARRY, who is standing with his back to her, paying the CLOAKROOM ATTENDANT and receiving his ticket. She rushes across to him, colliding with a

*hard-faced, peroxide woman in a dress covered in sequins.
RUTH mumbles a hasty apology and the woman glares after
her. She reaches the cloakroom counter just as LARRY turns
away from it.*

RUTH: Larry …

LARRY: Did you get your handbag … (*Seeing RUTH's
          expression*) What is it?

RUTH: (*Quickly*) Larry – that photograph … You
          remember the two people in the photograph …

LARRY: Yes?

RUTH: (*Excitedly*) I've just seen them!

LARRY: (*Astonished*) You've what?

*RUTH squeezes his arm as she looks towards the entrance.
LARRY follows her gaze. Two people come into the entrance
hall – a man and a woman. They are easily recognisable as
the two people in the photograph – referred to by LARRY's
brother as SEAN REYNOLDS and his wife. They stand in the
doorway for a moment, smiling happily.*

END OF EPISODE THREE

EPISODE FOUR

OPEN TO: The Foyer of the Imperial Hotel.

RUTH and LARRY are standing in the foyer looking towards the main entrance. Two people come into the entrance hall – a man and a woman. The couple are easily recognisable as the two people in the photograph – referred to by LARRY's brother as "SEAN REYNOLDS and his wife". They stand in the doorway for a moment, smiling happily.

RUTH: I'm right, aren't I, Larry? It is them?

LARRY: Yes, it's the couple in the photograph all right … (*Turning to look at her; quietly*) He's coming this way …

The man's name is NORMAN STANSDALE and the woman is FREDA STANSDALE. LARRY and RUTH face one another as NORMAN approaches. For a moment it looks as if he is coming to greet LARRY, but he walks past them to the cloakroom counter. FREDA crosses to the trestle to look at the poster advertising the band. When NORMAN sees the attendant is not at the cloakroom counter, he raps the counter. He looks around and sees LARRY and RUTH looking at him.

NORMAN: Where's the old boy got to?

LARRY: Oh – er – he was there a moment ago.

FREDA: Hey, I thought you said it was Jackie Munro ….

NORMAN: It is, isn't it?

FREDA: No. It's Monty Fry and the Frymen. It'll be all twist and rock.

NORMAN: Never mind, love. (*He winks at LARRY*) You can always untwist in the bar.

LARRY smiles. The CLOAKROOM ATTENDANT appears at the cloakroom counter. NORMAN turns to him.

NORMAN: Hello, Fred! Wondered where you'd got to. (*Handing over his overcoat*) Take special care of this one, will you? Savile Row – cost me a fortune.

FRED chuckles and takes the overcoat.

LARRY: (*To RUTH; quietly*) Later on, try and get friendly with his wife.

RUTH: Yes, all right.   I'm just going to get my handbag out of the car.

LARRY nods. RUTH glances in NORMAN's direction and goes, moving to the main entrance. NORMAN picks up his ticket and then crosses to FREDA. He takes her by the arm and escorts her into the dance hall. LARRY stands watching them as they enter the dance hall.

CUT TO: The Bar at the Dance. About an hour later.

This is an anteroom which has been transformed into a bar for the occasion.

A Barmaid and Barman are serving drinks behind the trestle table. Crates of beer, soft drinks, etc are stacked beneath the table, and seated at one of them is the busty, blonde singer we saw on the poster. She is playing the sophisticated star for the benefit of three teenage admirers, although she is obviously not a day over eighteen. The music of the dance band is heard blaring through the open door through which people pass to and from the dance hall. Last year's Christmas decorations have been brought out for the occasion and add to the general air of jolly depression. LARRY is seated at a table, smoking a cigarette, a half glass of beer before him. He is watching the blonde singer with faint amusement. He glances at his watch and looks towards the entrance of the dance hall. As he does so, LUTHER HARRIS enters from the dance hall. He glances around, sees LARRY, and crosses to him. LARRY pulls out a chair for LUTHER as he comes to the table.

LUTHER: Hello, Larry! Sorry I'm late. Peggy's not too good and I've got to take her home.

LARRY: Oh – I'm sorry to hear that. What's the trouble?

LUTHER: She's got a migraine; it started on the way here. (*Irritatedly*) It's always the same, old boy. Every time we go out she gets one of these wretched things.

LARRY: Well – she's got my sympathy. Let me get you a drink, Luther.

LUTHER: No, I won't, old chap, if you don't mind. What was it you wanted to see me about, Larry? Was it anything special, because if it wasn't … (*Glances at his watch*)

LARRY: No, I just wanted to have a chat, that's all.

LUTHER: It was terrible news about Phil. I just couldn't believe it.

LARRY: (*Quietly*) I don't believe it, Luther.

LUTHER looks at him, puzzled.

LARRY: Phil didn't commit suicide – he was murdered.

LUTHER: (*Quietly*) Is that what the police think?

LARRY: It's what I think.

LUTHER: Yes, well, if I were in your shoes, I'd think the same – especially after what happened to Andy Wilson. That was a very funny business.

LARRY: Yes, it certainly was. Do you think it has something to do with –?

LUTHER: With Phil?

LARRY: Yes.

LUTHER: Why, of course – don't you? It's too big a coincidence. Phil died under unusual circumstances and then someone tries to kill his best friend. (*Shaking his head*) Those boys were mixed up in something, Larry. They must have been! (*Quietly*) God knows what it was, though …

LARRY: I understand you've seen Andy?

LUTHER: Yes, I popped in the hospital to see how he was and they said I could have a chat with him. "Chat"'s a bit of an exaggeration – he only said half a dozen words. (*Puzzled*) Larry, have you any idea what this is all about?

LARRY: No, I haven't – but I intend to find out.

LUTHER looks at his watch again.

LUTHER: (*About to leave*) Well, if you ever feel I can help you, old boy – you know where I am.

LARRY: Thank you, Luther. (*Stopping him*) Oh, there is one thing. Did Phil ever mention going down to Maidenhead to you, at any time?

LUTHER: No. (*Thoughtfully*) No, I'm sure he didn't. Incidentally, why did he go to Maidenhead? What was he doing there?

LARRY: I don't know.

LUTHER: What was the name of the hotel?

LARRY: The Royal Falcon.

LUTHER: Is that the one just before you get to the bridge?

LARRY: No, it's over the bridge, on the other side. It's owned by a woman called Vanessa Curtis, but she has a manager – a rather pompous chap called Douglas Talbot.

LUTHER: I've never heard of either of them.

LARRY: No, I don't expect you have. (*Casually*) Have you heard of a man called Fletcher, by any chance?

LUTHER: Fletcher?

LARRY: Yes.

LUTHER: No, I don't think so.

LARRY: (*Quite pleasantly*) Well, he's heard of you.

He takes the dance card out of his pocket.

LARRY: He broke into my studio and during a struggle dropped his wallet. This ticket was inside. (*Turns over the ticket*) It's got three names scribbled on it. (*Reading from the card*) Phil Martin … Andy Wilson … (*Looking up*) Luther Harris …

LUTHER: (*With almost a suggestion of annoyance*) Why should my name be on that ticket?

LARRY: I don't know why. I was hoping you'd be able to tell me.

LUTHER: (*With almost a touch of indignation*) I've never heard of anyone called Fletcher. What did he look like, this man?

LARRY: He was about thirty-three or four; medium height, dark swarthy looking … He wore a double-breasted raincoat and was pretty handy with a knife.

LUTHER: Handy with a knife?

LARRY: Yes. He threw one at me.

LUTHER: But this is incredible; I mean … (*Shaking his head*) I've never heard of this chap – and I certainly don't know what my name was doing on that ticket, I'm damned if I do! Have you seen Andy Wilson?

LARRY: Yes.

LUTHER: Did you tell him about this? Did you ask him about Fletcher?

LARRY: No …

LUTHER: (*Surprised; almost aggressive in manner*) Well – why not?

LARRY: Because it wasn't until after I'd seen Andy that I had the pleasure of meeting the gentleman.

LUTHER: Well, if I were you, I'd show Andy that ticket and ask him whether he knows Fletcher. And if he does, ask him to find out what the hell my name's doing on that ticket!

LARRY: That's a good idea. I'll probably do that.

LUTHER: Larry, I must fly! I don't want to keep Peggy
              waiting any longer.
LARRY: Yes, of course.
LUTHER: Goodbye, Larry.

*LUTHER turns and leaves the table, crossing towards the
dance hall. NORMAN STANSDALE appears from the other
end of the room. He is carrying a glass of beer and a gin and
tonic and is obviously looking for his wife. As he turns
towards the bar to put the drinks down, FREDA STANSDALE
and RUTH come out of the door marked "Powder Room".
RUTH and FREDA have obviously become acquainted and
are enjoying a private little joke. NORMAN crosses to them.*

NORMAN: (*To FREDA*) What happened to you?
FREDA: What do you think happened? I went to spend
              a penny. (*To RUTH*) He hasn't got much
              imagination, has he? (*Notices drink*) Is that
              for me?
NORMAN: (*With a wink at RUTH*) No – Brigitte Bardot
              …

FREDA laughs and takes the drink from NORMAN.

FREDA: (*To RUTH*) Did I give you back the lipstick?
RUTH: Yes, thanks.
NORMAN: (*Smiling at RUTH*) Blimey, has she been
              borrowing again?

*RUTH crosses to LARRY, who has been watching them with
interest. There are several vacant chairs at LARRY's table
and RUTH sits down on one of them.*

LARRY: (*Quietly*) Who are they?
RUTH: The name's Stansdale – they're married.
LARRY: Ask them to join us, Ruth.

*Ruth nods and looks across at FREDA and NORMAN who
are standing drinking and laughing.*

RUTH: (*Calling*) Why don't you join us?
FREDA: Yes – that's a good idea …

FREDA and NORMAN cross to LARRY's table. LARRY rises.

FREDA: (*To RUTH*) These shoes are killing me. I wish to God I'd bought a size larger.

LARRY takes out his cigarette case and offers FREDA and NORMAN a cigarette.

FREDA: No, thanks.

NORMAN: Ta.

RUTH refuses a cigarette; as they all sit down LARRY lights NORMAN's cigarette for him.

RUTH: (*To NORMAN*) Are you on leave?

NORMAN: Yes, I go back on Tuesday. Worse luck!

FREDA: Don't let him kid you. That's for my benefit- he loves it!

NORMAN grins at LARRY and winks.

RUTH: (*To LARRY; sadly*) Wasn't poor old Phil going back on Tuesday?

LARRY realises what RUTH is doing.

LARRY: Yes, I think he was.

RUTH: (*To Norman*) That's a friend of mine. He was in the Army – he committed suicide. You probably read about it.

FREDA: (*Surprised*) That wasn't the chap at Maidenhead?

RUTH: That's right.

NORMAN looks at his wife, then at RUTH.

NORMAN: Philip Martin?

RUTH: Yes.

NORMAN: He was a friend of yours, then?

RUTH: Yes – a very dear friend.

NORMAN: Well, I'm damned! (*To FREDA*) It only goes to show, doesn't it? It's a small world!

LARRY: Why? Did you know Philip Martin?

NORMAN: No, I've never met him. But funnily enough, we've met his brother.

LARRY: (*Taken aback*) His brother?

FREDA: Yes – Larry Martin. He's a photographer. He's very well known. There was quite a bit in the papers about him when his brother died.

NORMAN: (*To RUTH*) I expect you know him, anyway, if you were pally with his brother.

RUTH: Yes, I know him.

FREDA: (*Amused: to RUTH*) He's a nut, isn't he? He really is …

LARRY looks at her, then at NORMAN.

LARRY: (*Quietly; to NORMAN*) When did you meet Larry Martin?

NORMAN: About six months ago. He took some pictures of us.

LARRY: (*Stunned*) Larry Martin did?

NORMAN: Yes.

LARRY: Where?

NORMAN: What do you mean – where?

LARRY: Where did he take the pictures?

NORMAN: (*Surprised by the question*) Why, in his studio, of course!

NORMAN stares at LARRY, faintly puzzled by his manner.

RUTH: (*Quickly; pleasantly*) I think I went there once. Phil took me. If I remember rightly it was near … (*She hesitates, pretending to give the matter thought*) … Oh dear, my memory …

FREDA: It's in Knightsbridge; in a mews, just off Hyde Park Corner.

RUTH: Yes, of course, that's right! Melton Mews … I remember now – there's a showcase on the wall   …

NORMAN: That's it – that's the place!

FREDA:	Go on, Norman, tell them about it – tell them what happened. It doesn't matter now, anyway ...
NORMAN:	(*With a little laugh*) Well – if you're really interested ...
LARRY:	We're interested.
NORMAN:	(*Amused*) It was a bloody funny business and no mistake ...
FREDA:	It was last February and Norman was on leave ...
NORMAN:	Just towards the end of my leave, as a matter of fact. (*Grinning*) And we were skint, absolutely skint. I don't think we'd got ten bob between us. Anyway, Freda and I were having a drink in a pub called The Four Jacks, it's just off the Strand. There was a dark, serious looking chap sitting up at the bar and after a moment he came over to our table and introduced himself. He said his name was Cliff Fletcher and that he worked for one of the big advertising agencies. He told us he was looking for a couple to feature in an advertisement and he had a pretty shrewd idea that Freda and I might fill the bill.
FREDA:	To cut a long story short he offered us fifty quid if we'd pose for the photograph. Naturally, we jumped at the idea.
NORMAN:	He gave us the address of the photographer and told us to be there at ten o'clock the next morning.

CUT TO: The showcase on the wall near the entrance of LARRY's flat. It contains PHILIP MARTIN's photograph as in Episode One.

NORMAN's VOICE: Of course we talked about nothing else all that night and the following morning Freda took so long dolling herself up we didn't get there until a quarter past ten.

Freda is standing near the showcase, gazing at it. NORMAN thrusts his wrist in front of FREDA's face, showing her the time on his wristwatch. FREDA gives a look of alarm. NORMAN hurries her in through the entrance to the flat.

CUT TO: Outside the front door of LARRY MARTIN's flat. As the following action takes place NORMAN's voice is heard over it.

NORMAN and FREDA wait nervously at the door. FLETCHER opens the door and smiles charmingly as NORMAN apologises for being late. NORMAN takes off his hat and follows FREDA through the door.

NORMAN's VOICE: Fletcher came to the door almost as soon as I rang the bell. I said we was sorry we were late, but Fletcher didn't seem at all put out. He said Mr Martin was ready for us – an' would we step inside, please. We stepped inside …

CUT TO: The Hall and Living Room of LARRY MARTIN's flat.

NORMAN and FREDA enter the hall. FLETCHER closes the door.

FLETCHER: If you'll come this way …

They follow him into the living room. They look in the direction of a person in the room, as yet unseen. FLETCHER introduces them.

FLETCHER: Mr and Mrs Stansdale … Mr Larry Martin.

FREDA smiles nervously.

NORMAN: Pleased to meet you.

The unseen person comes into shot, moving to them. It is
THOMAS QUAYLE.

THOMAS: How do you do?

He studies them in silence for a moment. NORMAN fidgets
with his hat.

THOMAS: Well, now – I don't know how much Mr
              Fletcher has told you …

NORMAN: Oh, he explained it all to us. You take the
              photographs – and we get the fifty pounds.

THOMAS: (*Smiling faintly*) Yes – well – it's not quite as
              simple as that, you know.

NORMAN looks suspicious. He glances quickly at FREDA.

NORMAN: Here we go. I thought this sounded a bit too
              good to be true. (*To THOMAS*) What's the
              catch?

THOMAS: Oh, there's no catch, Mr Stansdale …

NORMAN: (*Truculently*) When do we get the fifty quid?

THOMAS looks at FLETCHER. FLETCHER smiles and takes
out his wallet. He counts out ten five-pound notes and   hands
them to NORMAN. NORMAN looks sheepishly from one to
the other.

NORMAN: Well – there was no need – I mean, after the
              job would've done. But when you said it
              wasn't quite as simple as all that …

THOMAS: What I meant, Mr Stansdale, was that it's not
              simply a matter of clicking the shutter and
              away you go. One has to get these things
              right. It takes time and a good deal of hard
              work, and as you're not professional models
              you may be here for the best part of the day.

NORMAN: Oh – I see what you mean. I'm sorry I …

THOMAS: That's all right. Let's make a start, shall we?
              We're all ready for you.

THOMAS leads the way into the studio. FREDA smiles quickly at FLETCHER and follows THOMAS. NORMAN looks around the room, turning to FLETCHER as he goes.

NORMAN: Nice place. There's money in this game, eh?

FLETCHER: Oh yes, indeed there is.

NORMAN stuffs the fifty pounds into his jacket pocket as he follows the others into the studio. FLETCHER looks after him with a slow smile. He reaches inside his breast pocket, taking out a folded sheet of paper. He opens the paper, studies it for a moment, then moves to the studio door, going in.

CUT TO: LARRY MARTIN's Studio.

This scene is played in silence as NORMAN's voice takes up the story once again.

The lights have been set up around a piano stool. FREDA, giggling nervously, is seated on the stool, holding an accordion which has been strapped to her shoulders. NORMAN is standing awkwardly beside her and a little behind her. THOMAS is talking to them, indicating the direction in which he wants them to look. (FREDA and NORMAN are, in fact, being placed in position for the "SEAN REYNOLDS photographs" already established) FLETCHER moves NORMAN nearer FREDA, then puts FREDA's hands on the keyboard of the accordion, taking great care with the placing of the fingers.

NORMAN's VOICE: We was very surprised when we discovered that Freda was to be photographed playing an accordion. I mean, she'd never played one in her life before. An' blimey, was Larry Martin a stickler for getting things right. He must have rearranged her hands about a couple of dozen times. He got it right in the end – for the first photograph that is.

FLETCHER, seated, cigarette in mouth, studies the sheet of paper he took from his pocket earlier in the scene. THOMAS leans over FLETCHER's shoulder, looking at the paper. FLETCHER indicates something on the paper. THOMAS nods thoughtfully.

NORMAN's VOICE: Then it all started all over again for the second one. Fletcher was there all the time – lookin' on and making suggestions to Larry Martin. I was getting really cheesed off round about twelve o'clock ... And when they told us they wasn't breakin' for lunch it didn't help to make my smiles more natural. They must have taken about thirty or forty photographs altogether and the same old palaver every time. There may be money in the game – but if they 'ave to go through that lot every time they take a photo – they can keep it. Frankly, I thought he was never goin' to finish.

THOMAS leans over FREDA and rearranges her hands on the keyboard of the accordion. He comes round to his camera, tells them to hold their position and takes the photograph. FLETCHER nods to THOMAS and folds up the paper in his hand signifying that the session is over.

NORMAN's VOICE: Then at about five o'clock he told us it was all over and that we could pack it in ...

NORMAN sighs with relief. FREDA unstraps the accordion assisted by NORMAN and then leans back when the instrument is on the floor, stretching her cramped fingers. NORMAN takes out a packet of cigarettes and lights one for her. She comments on the stiffness of her fingers to NORMAN as she takes the cigarette from him.

NORMAN's VOICE: I was absolutely shagged; and poor old Freda – her 'ands were that stiff she could hardly 'old a cigarette …

CUT TO: The Bar at the Dance. As before.
FREDA, NORMAN, RUTH and LARRY are in relatively the same positions as they were when NORMAN commenced his story.

LARRY: … And I take it you never saw Larry Martin again?

NORMAN: No. We didn't see him again from that day to this. Once my leave was over, o' course, I forgot the whole business.

LARRY: Did you ever see any of the photographs?

FREDA: No, at least, <u>I</u> didn't …

NORMAN: I didn't either, until a couple of days ago. (*To FREDA*) Day before yesterday, wasn't it, Freda?

FREDA: Yes, that's right.

LARRY: What happened the day before yesterday?

NORMAN: I went down to Aldershot to see a couple o' friends of mine. Hadn't seem 'em for ages. We was playin' darts in the local when a chap suddenly walks in and shows me one of the photographs. I've never been so surprised in my life.

LARRY: Go on …

NORMAN: He asked me where the photograph was taken, how much I was paid, and all the rest of it. Bowled me over, I can tell you. I got the wind up proper.

LARRY: Who was this man? Did he tell you his name?

NORMAN: No, he didn't, but the bloke behind the bar seemed to know 'im. He said his name was Hyde, Chief Inspector Hyde.

LARRY glances at RUTH. FREDA sees the look and becomes curious at the alarm on RUTH's face.

LARRY: (*Looking at NORMAN: slowly*) And you told Chief Inspector Hyde that the photographs were taken by Larry Martin?

NORMAN: Yes, of course I did! What else could I tell 'im?

LARRY nods, then rises abruptly from the table.

LARRY: If you'll excuse me … (*To RUTH*) I'll be back in a moment.

LARRY goes toward the dance hall. NORMAN stares after him, then turns to look bewilderedly at FREDA, who is distinctly suspicious of LARRY by now – and a little unnerved by his sudden departure.

CUT TO: *A small bookcase with a telephone on the top shelf. The telephone is ringing. HYDE enters and lifts the receiver. He is eating a sandwich and has been resting: he wears an old dressing gown.*

HYDE: Hello? …

CUT TO: A telephone cubicle at the Imperial Hotel. *LARRY is in the cubicle: he is tense and agitated. On hearing HYDE's voice he presses button "A"*

LARRY: Hello? Is that you, Hyde?

HYDE's VOICE: (*Pleasantly*) Speaking …

LARRY: This is Larry Martin.

For the rest of this conversation we cut back and forth to where the person speaking is.

HYDE: Oh, good evening, Mr Martin.

LARRY: (*Angrily*) Listen – I've got to see you! It's important – very important!

HYDE: (*Casually*) I'll drop in tomorrow morning, Mr Martin – about eleven o'clock.

LARRY: No, you don't understand! This is urgent – I've got to see you tonight!

HYDE: (*Unperturbed*) Tomorrow morning, Mr Martin. Eleven o'clock. Thank you for ringing …

HYDE slowly replaces the receiver: There is a suggestion of a smile on his face as he continues to eat his sandwich.

CUT TO: The living room of LARRY MARTIN's flat. It is the following morning.

RUTH comes out of the studio, carrying a tray with several cups on it: she puts the tray down on the desk, then opens a drawer and takes out a large envelope. She is returning to the studio when the doorbell rings. RUTH goes out into the hall. She opens the front door to find INSPECTOR HYDE on the threshold.

HYDE: (*Pleasantly*) Good morning, Miss Sanders. I have an appointment with Mr Martin …

RUTH: Yes – come in, Inspector.

HYDE enters and crosses the hall to enter the living room, followed by RUTH.

RUTH: I'll tell Mr Martin you're here.

She goes into the studio. HYDE nods, and crossing to the window stands looking down into the mews. After a little while RUTH returns: she is now carrying a photograph as well as the envelope.

RUTH: Mr Martin will be with you in a moment.

HYDE: (*Turning; smiling at RUTH*) Thank you.

RUTH puts the photograph in the envelope, and taking a pen and some Sellotape, prepares the package for the post. HYDE watches her.

HYDE: Did you enjoy the dance last night, Miss Sanders?

RUTH turns, surprised by the question.

RUTH: Er – yes, thank you.

HYDE smiles. LARRY comes out of the studio. He looks across at the INSPECTOR. He is obviously still annoyed: his manner tense and a little abrupt. He speaks to RUTH whilst still looking at HYDE.

LARRY: Carol's having trouble with her dress – give her a hand, Ruth.

RUTH nods and with a glance at HYDE, goes into the studio.

HYDE: (*Pleasantly*) Good morning, Mr Martin. I understand you want to see me?

LARRY: You're darn right I want to see you! Now, Inspector – what the hell are you playing at?

HYDE: (*Unruffled*) I didn't know I was playing at anything, sir?

LARRY: The last time you came here you showed me the photograph …

HYDE: That's right, sir.

LARRY: You asked me if I knew the people in the photograph …

HYDE: That's right, sir. You said you didn't.

LARRY: Yes, and all the time you were convinced – a hundred per cent convinced – that not only did I know them but that I'd actually taken the blasted photograph!

HYDE: Oh, I was convinced of that, was I, sir?

LARRY: Yes, of course you were! You must have been!

HYDE: Did you take the photograph?

LARRY: No, of course I didn't! But I don't expect you to believe …

HYDE: But I do believe you, Mr Martin. Now I suggest you calm down, sir, and listen to my side of the story. When Stansdale told me what happened I

109

realised that you had either been lying to me or someone had taken the trouble to impersonate you. That's why I showed you the photograph again – to give you the chance to change your story.

(*Shaking his head*) But you didn't change it, so I made certain enquiries. The first thing I discovered was that you couldn't possibly have taken the photograph because …

LARRY: I was in Bermuda.

HYDE: (*Smiling*) Exactly.

He takes an envelope out of his pocket and glances at it.

HYDE: You arrived in Bermuda on February the 3rd and left on the 29th. You stayed at the Ocean Beach Hotel and occupied Suite 102.

LARRY: (*Relieved*) Well, thank God for that! I thought …

HYDE: Yes. I know what you thought, sir. But if you'll forgive my saying so, you really oughtn't to be quite so – one hundred per cent certain about things, Mr Martin.

LARRY smiles.

HYDE: Now, sir, I'd like you to tell me about last night.

LARRY: Last night?

HYDE: Yes – the dance. Why did you go there, Mr Martin?

LARRY: I found a dance ticket and was curious. You see, Phil told me he intended to go to a dance last night and I wondered if this was the same one.

HYDE: Where did you find the ticket?

LARRY: In Fletcher's wallet.

HYDE: (*Surprised*) When did you see Fletcher?

LARRY: The night before last.

He crosses to the desk and takes FLETCHER's knife and the dance ticket out of the drawer.

LARRY: When I got back from the hospital he was here, searching the flat. That woman was with him, the one I saw in Arundel: Mrs Seldon.

HYDE: Go on …

LARRY: I tried to stop Fletcher but he had a knife and got the better of me. During the struggle he dropped his wallet. The dance ticket was inside.

HYDE looks at LARRY and he takes the knife and examines it.

HYDE: You should have told me about this at the time.

LARRY: Yes, I know I should. But when I found the ticket …

HYDE: Is that the ticket?

LARRY hands HYDE the dance ticket.

LARRY: Yes. There's three names scribbled on the back of it. My brother's – Andy Wilson's – and Luther Harris's. That's why I went to the dance, Inspector; I wanted to see if Luther was there.

HYDE: (*Quietly*) And was he?

LARRY: Yes, he was.

LARRY is faintly perturbed now: not sure whether HYDE believes him or not.

HYDE: Did you tell him about the ticket?

LARRY: Yes – but he couldn't understand why his name was on it. He said he'd never heard of anyone called Fletcher.

HYDE looks at LARRY then at the ticket.

HYDE: What was Fletcher and this woman looking for, do you know?

LARRY: Yes – the key …

HYDE: You mean Mrs Curtis's key – the one you gave me?

LARRY: Yes. (*Hesitates*) You see – I had a duplicate made and they apparently knew about it.

HYDE: (*Curious*) Why did you do that, Mr Martin?

111

LARRY: After I'd seen Mrs Curtis at Datchet, I came to the conclusion that the key was important, so …

HYDE: You had a copy made?

LARRY: Yes.

HYDE: Do you think that was the correct thing to do, under the circumstances?

LARRY: Yes, I do, because I'm not yet convinced that the other didn't belong to my brother.

HYDE: Well, if it did belong to him, sir, it means he had a key to Mrs Curtis's apartment. I saw Mrs Curtis this morning. She told me it was her key and she gave me permission to try it. It was hers all right.

LARRY: (*Disappointed*) Oh, I see.

HYDE crosses towards the hall.

HYDE: How did you get on with Andy Wilson?

LARRY: Not very well. He refused to talk.

HYDE nods, obviously not surprised.

HYDE: He didn't say anything, sir?

LARRY: He told me to stop interfering and mind my own business.

HYDE: Did he say what would happen if you don't, sir?

LARRY: He gave me a pretty good idea.

HYDE: Yes, well, I don't doubt you can look after yourself, Mr Martin. But try not to drag other people into this affair if you can possibly help it, sir. (*Turning, smiling at LARRY*) Say goodbye to Miss Sanders for me, sir. Charming girl …

He goes out into the hall. Larry is puzzled by the Inspector's reference to Ruth and stares across at the studio door.

CUT TO: LARRY MARTIN's Studio.

LARRY is working – taking photographs of SALLY NARES, a very pretty girl in her early twenties. SALLY is wearing a mink stole and is obviously posing for a fashion magazine

112

feature. The telephone rings in the living room. It stops and after a moment RUTH enters.

RUTH: I'm sorry, Larry – Luther Harris is on the phone and insists on having a word with you.

LARRY: (*Surprised*) Luther?

RUTH: Yes.

LARRY: All right, Ruth. (*To SALLY*) I shan't be a minute, Sally. Relax.

With a sigh of relief, SALLY relaxes. RUTH smiles at her.

CUT TO: The Living Room of LARRY MARTIN's flat.
LARRY enters and crosses to the telephone on the desk.

LARRY: (*On phone*) Hello, Luther? Larry …

CUT TO: A Telephone Box in a London Square.
For the rest of this conversation we cut back and forth between the two settings. LUTHER HARRIS is in the box, waiting for LARRY to come to the phone.

LUTHER: (*On hearing LARRY's voice*) Larry – I'm sorry to disturb you, but it is rather important …

LARRY: What is it, Luther?

LUTHER: I've just seen Andy Wilson and I thought I ought to have a word with you, Larry.

LARRY: Why? What's happened?

LUTHER: Nothing's happened – but … I've got something to tell you – about Phil … I think it's important, Larry.

LARRY: Well – where are you? Where are you speaking from?

LUTHER: I'm in a box – just opposite the hospital. Could you pick me up, Larry?

LARRY: (*A sudden decision*) Yes, I'll be there in fifteen minutes.

CUT TO: A London Square.

*LARRY's car approaches and as it pulls into the curb
LUTHER HARRIS appears from the far side of the box.
LARRY leans across and opens the door. LUTHER gets into
the car and it drives off.*

CUT TO: Inside LARRY MARTIN's car.

LARRY is driving; LUTHER HARRIS is seated alongside him.

LARRY: Now what's all this about, Luther?

LUTHER: When I last saw Andy, he asked me to get him a
         book – a book on jazz. It's a new one, just out.

LARRY: Well?

LUTHER: I was passing the hospital this afternoon, so I
         dropped it in on him.

LARRY: Go on …

LUTHER takes a ticket out of his waistcoat pocket.

LUTHER: He seemed perfectly all right, very much better, in
         fact – then just as I was leaving, he produced this
         and asked me to do him a favour.

LARRY: (*Glancing at the ticket*) What is it?

LUTHER: It's a left-luggage ticket – Victoria Station.

LARRY: Go on, Luther.

LUTHER: He told me Phil had deposited a case at Victoria
         and given him the ticket. He asked me to get the
         case and keep it at my place.

LARRY: Is it Phil's case?

LUTHER: Presumably. I asked him why he didn't keep the
         ticket and he said that he was worried about it and
         he wanted me to look after it until he came out of
         hospital.

LARRY: Why didn't he give me the ticket if the case
         belongs to Phil?

LUTHER: Yes, that's just it, Larry. (*Shaking his head*) He
         said there were several letters of his in the case

114

and he wanted to take them out before he gave it to you.

LARRY: Then he did intend to hand the case over to me?

LUTHER: Well – that's what he said. (*Nervously*) Look, Larry – I'll be frank with you. I made a mistake. I shouldn't have taken the ticket. The police have already questioned me about your brother and Andy Wilson. I don't want to get too involved in this business.

LARRY: I understand, Luther. I'll take the ticket.

LUTHER hands LARRY the ticket.

LUTHER: What will you do, give it to the police?

LARRY: I don't know. If it is Phil's case I'd like to know what's in it.

LUTHER: Yes, only …

LARRY: Only what?

LUTHER: Be careful, Larry …

LARRY looks at LUTHER.

CUT TO: LUTHER HARRIS's Record Shop.

LARRY's car pulls up outside of the shop and LUTHER HARRIS gets out. He nods to LARRY and moves to the shop door. LARRY's car pulls away from the kerb.

CUT TO: The Left-Luggage Office at Victoria Station.

A Man takes two heavy suitcases from the counter and moves off. LARRY, who has been waiting behind him, moves to the counter and gives the CLERK his ticket. LARRY glances around and after a moment or two the CLERK returns. He puts the attaché case on the counter. LARRY pays the CLERK and picks up the case. He hesitates for a moment, feeling the weight of it. It is obviously very heavy. He sees the CLERK looking at him with a curious expression. He smiles quickly and moves towards the entrance.

115

CUT TO: Outside Victoria Station.
LARRY's car is parked near the station entrance. He arrives at the car, opens the door, puts the case on the passenger seat, and gets into the driving seat.

CUT TO: Inside LARRY MARTIN's car.
LARRY is looking down at the case. The locks are facing upwards. LARRY tries to open it, pressing the spring catches. It is locked. He remains there for a moment, looking at the case with a puzzled expression. He sighs and starts the engine of the car.

CUT TO: LARRY MARTIN's front door.
LARRY puts down the case, takes out his door key, and opens the front door. He picks up the case and goes in.

CUT TO: The hall and living room of LARRY MARTIN's flat.
RUTH's voice is heard on the telephone from the living room.
RUTH's VOICE: Yes, I will – as soon as he gets in …
LARRY closes the door and moves to the living room taking the case with him. RUTH is at the telephone. She is in her street clothes and there are several large envelopes, ready for posting, on the desk in front of her. She was obviously just leaving as the telephone rang. Larry enters.
RUTH: (*Into telephone*) Goodbye …
LARRY enters as RUTH replaces the receiver.
RUTH: Oh – that was Inspector Hyde …
LARRY: What does he want?
LARRY puts down the case. RUTH stares at it for a moment before replying.
RUTH: They've just picked up a man – they think it's Cliff Fletcher.
LARRY: Fletcher!

RUTH: He's at Chelsea Police Station. They want you to
          go round there and identify him. They're sending
          a police car.

LARRY: I see. Did they say where they'd picked him up?

RUTH: No.

LARRY nods. RUTH is still staring at the case.

RUTH: What's that?

LARRY: It belonged to Phil. It was in the Left-Luggage at
          Victoria.

*He is obviously waiting for RUTH to leave; he indicates the
envelopes on the desk.*

LARRY: Don't miss the post, Ruth.

RUTH smiles faintly, getting the message.

RUTH: I've still got that stuff for the Delton Agency to
          finish off. I was popping out for something to eat
          and coming back later – if that's all right.

LARRY: Yes, of course. See you later, then.

*RUTH takes up the envelopes, and glances once again at the
case.*

RUTH: Goodbye.

LARRY: Goodbye, Ruth …

*RUTH goes out. As soon as he hears the front door closing,
LARRY takes up the case and puts it down on the settee. He
takes off his coat and throws it over a chair. He takes a bunch
of keys from his pocket and tries to unlock the case. None of
them fits. He moves quickly to the studio, returning the keys to
his pocket. After a moment, LARRY returns carrying a heavy
screwdriver. He bends over the case, inserts the screwdriver
between the spring catch and the side of the case, attempting
to prise open the catch. He applies pressure but nothing
happens. He tries again and this time the catch flies open. He
repeats the performance on the second catch, eventually
prising that one open. He puts down the screwdriver, lays the
case down flat, and opens it. LARRY stares down at the case*

in astonishment. It is filled with bundles of bank notes –
German Deutsche Marks. LARRY takes up one of the bundles,
looks at it, throws it down onto the settee. A thought strikes
him. He empties the contents down onto the settee, searching
amongst the bundles of notes. There is nothing else there. He
straightens up, lighting a cigarette as he glances thoughtfully
down at the money and the empty case. There is the sound of
a car in the mews below. LARRY remembers that HYDE is
calling for him. With a look of alarm, he crosses to the
window, looking down into the mews. He sees the car
continue driving down the mews. LARRY looks relieved. He
goes back to the settee and starts to put the notes back into
the case.

CUT TO: The Front Door of LARRY MARTIN's flat.
A burly figure stands at the door, his finger on the doorbell.
He is EDDIE MEADOWS, a healthy, rugger playing type,
about thirty-two, dressed in overcoat and trilby hat.

CUT TO: The   Hall   and   Living   Room   of   LARRY
MARTIN's flat.
LARRY comes from the living room, going to the front door.
He is putting on his overcoat. The attaché case is now
standing on the floor near the hall stand. LARRY opens the
front door.

MEADOWS: Good evening, sir. Mr Larry Martin?
LARRY: That's right.
MEADOWS: Inspector Hyde telephoned you, sir, to ask
                   you to …
LARRY: That's right, I'm just coming.
LARRY turns back into the hall to pick up the attaché case.
LARRY: I've got something to show the Inspector.
MEADOWS: Oh? What's that, sir?
LARRY pats the attaché case as he moves to the front door.

LARRY: Just this …

MEADOWS looks bewildered at the attaché case as LARRY comes out and makes to close the door.

MEADOWS: What's in it, sir?

Just as LARRY is on the point of replying the telephone rings in the flat.

LARRY: Oh – excuse me a moment, will you?

LARRY goes into the flat. MEADOWS remains there, looking after him. LARRY puts down the attaché case and goes to the desk. He takes up the telephone receiver.

LARRY: Hello? …

HYDE's VOICE: Mr Martin? …

LARRY: Speaking …

HYDE's VOICE: Inspector Hyde here …

LARRY: Oh, yes – I'm just on my way, Inspector …

HYDE's VOICE: On your way?

LARRY: That's right. Your man's just arrived.

HYDE's VOICE: My man? What are you talking about?

LARRY: You phoned about twenty minutes ago to say
              that you'd picked up Cliff Fletcher …

HYDE's VOICE: I phoned you?

LARRY: Not me, my secretary. She said you wanted
              me to come to Chelsea Police Station to
              identify …

LARRY's voice trails away. He has heard a slight sound behind him. He turns sharply. EDDIE MEADOWS is standing behind him, a gun in his hand.

LARRY: What the …

MEADOWS: Put it down.

LARRY stares at the gun. MEADOWS makes a threatening movement. HYDE's voice is heard at the other end of the line.

HYDE's VOICE: Hello? Mr Martin? Mr Martin, are you
              there?

119

Slowly LARRY replaces the receiver. MEADOWS indicates the attaché case.

MEADOWS: Pick it up.

LARRY: Look, what's going on …?

MEADOWS: Move!

LARRY picks up the case.

MEADOWS: Now – I believe you have a key we want, Mr Martin.

LARRY: Who the hell are <u>you</u>?

MEADOWS: The key, please!

LARRY hesitates. An ugly expression comes over MEADOWS's face. He is obviously not a man to make idle threats. Slowly, LARRY puts his hand in his pocket and takes out the key. He makes to give it to MEADOWS – then hesitates.

LARRY: Just tell me, will you? Why is this so important – to so many people?

MEADOWS simply holds out his hand for the key. With a clumsy movement, LARRY drops the key. MEADOWS smiles grimly, not taking his eyes off LARRY for a second.

MEADOWS: Pick it up.

LARRY shrugs lightly.

LARRY: If you insist on …

On the word 'Insist' LARRY lashes out with the attaché case at MEADOWS's gun-hand. MEADOWS curses as the gun flies across the room. LARRY is thrown off balance by the movement and half falls on to one knee. EDDIE moves to him, a vicious right arm appraised. LARRY rises to meet him, at the same time flinging his arm in an outward upward movement. The attaché case catches MEADOWS flush in the face. He reels backwards, falling into the settee. LARRY drops the case, scrambles for the gun and picks it up. MEADOWS rises to find himself facing the gun in LARRY's hand. They stand in silence for a moment, both breathing heavily. LARRY looks at the key on the floor. Carefully he bends and picks it up. He holds it up, looking at MEADOWS.

LARRY: Now – let's have it. Why do you want this?

MEADOWS: I don't know – I was just told to get it, that's all.

LARRY: Who sent you here?

MEADOWS looks at him stubbornly. A thought occurs to LARRY. He moves to the window: keeping a watchful eye on MEADOWS. He parts the curtains and looks down into the mews. A car is parked near the entrance to LARRY's flat. The driving seat window is open and the right arm and shoulder of a MAN can be seen in the driving seat. He flicks ash from his cigarette out of the open window. LARRY smiles faintly and turns to MEADOWS.

LARRY: So you have a friend with you?

MEADOWS: (*Frightened*) Look – let me clear out of here. Don't get mixed up with him, because if you do …

LARRY: Who is he?

MEADOWS doesn't reply.

LARRY: All right – we'll let him introduce himself. He's going to get curious sooner or later. We may as well be comfortable while we're waiting.

LARRY indicates the settee. Reluctantly, MEADOWS sits. LARRY sits in the armchair, after turning it slightly to face the door.

CUT TO: Outside of LARRY MARTIN's Flat in the Mews.
The MAN's arm comes out through the open driver's window and tosses away the cigarette end. The car door opens, and the MAN gets out. As he turns to look at the flat entrance we see that he is CLIFF FLETCHER.

CUT TO: LARRY MARTIN's flat.

MEADOWS and LARRY are seated as before, waiting for FLETCHER. MEADOWS looks nervous. LARRY watches him, glancing towards the door as he appears to hear a noise outside the flat.

MEADOWS: (*Quietly*) That's him …

They both stare in the direction of the open hall door. LARRY turns the gun away from MEADOWS, pointing at the doorway. They sit there, waiting for FLETCHER to appear …

END OF EPISODE FOUR

EPISODE FIVE

OPEN TO: The Living Room of LARRY MARTIN's flat.
EDDIE MEADOWS is seated on the settee, looking nervously in LARRY's direction. LARRY is in the armchair opposite him, gun in hand. LARRY appears to hear a noise outside the flat. They both stare in the direction of the open hall door. LARRY turns the gun away from EDDIE pointing it at the doorway.

CUT TO: The Ground Floor entrance to the flats.
CLIFF FLETCHER is approaching the foot of the stairs. He hesitates on the stairs. He has second thoughts about going in. He cannot understand why MEADOWS hasn't returned with LARRY as arranged. He looks up again, then back at his car, seen outside, through the entrance. He remains there, indecisively, looking up, and then suddenly, he returns to the car, gets into the driving seat and slams the door shut.

CUT TO: The Living Room of LARRY MARTIN's flat.
LARRY and MEADOWS are seated as before, staring at the hall doorway. The sound of FLETCHER's car is heard starting up in the mews below. LARRY and MEADOWS look sharply towards the window. LARRY crosses to the window, looking down into the mews, following the car with his eyes at it drives away.

LARRY: Well – it looks as if you friend is leaving you to face the music.

LARRY turns to MEADOWS and sees the settee is empty. MEADOWS has taken advantage of the moment of relaxed vigilance: he is already moving to the front door. LARRY runs to the hall doorway in pursuit. MEADOWS runs out through the front doorway, just as LARRY comes out of the living room. LARRY chases after him.

CUT TO: The Entrance to the MEWS.

FLETCHER's car comes out of the mews and turns into the main road. As it races off down the road, a police car comes from the opposite direction. The police car slows and turns into the mews and pulls up outside of LARRY's flat. HYDE gets out of the car, followed by TWO PLAIN CLOTHES MEN. EDDIE MEADOWS rushes out of the entrance to the flat. He stands there for a second, alarmed and surprised to find the police facing him. As HYDE moves towards him, he runs down the mews exit. HYDE and the two PLAIN CLOTHES MEN chase after him. LARRY comes out of the flat entrance and stands there staring after them. One of the PLAIN CLOTHES MEN overtakes HYDE and tackles MEADOWS just as he reaches the exit to the mews. They fall to the ground. MEADOWS struggles to free himself. The other MAN joins them, and MEADOWS is pulled to his feet. HYDE comes breathlessly up to them, followed by LARRY. HYDE looks at MEADOWS, obviously recognising him.

HYDE: Well, I'm damned – Eddie Meadows! We've
           been looking for you, Eddie. (*He looks at
           LARRY*) You seem to have some interesting
           friends, Mr Martin. I think you'd better come
           along with us and tell me all about them.

LARRY: All right, Inspector. But first – I've got
           something upstairs which might interest you.

HYDE looks at LARRY with curiosity.

CUT TO: The Living Room of LARRY MARTIN's flat.
The attaché case is open on the settee revealing the money. HYDE stands looking down at it. He looks at the bundle of notes in his hand and tosses it into the case. He looks across at LARRY who is lighting a cigarette.

HYDE: Let's get this straight. Andy Wilson gave Luther
           Harris a left-luggage ticket – and Luther Harris
           gave it to you?

LARRY: That's right.

HYDE: H'm … If the case belonged to your brother why
           didn't Andy Wilson give you the ticket?

LARRY: There were supposed to be some things in it that
           belonged to Andy. He wanted to take them out
           before handing the case over to me.

HYDE: I see. And why did Luther Harris decide to hand
           the ticket to you?

LARRY: He said he was afraid of getting mixed up in
           something. You'd already questioned him about
           Phil and Andy Wilson …

HYDE: If he was frightened of getting mixed up in
           something why did he accept the ticket in the
           first place?

LARRY shrugs.

LARRY: I don't know. Perhaps he got cold feet at the last
           minute.

*HYDE looks thoughtfully down at the case for a moment
before continuing.*

HYDE: This phone call – the one I was supposed to have
           made … What did they say?

LARRY: Just that you'd picked up Cliff Fletcher and you
           wanted me to identify him. My secretary took the
           call. She said you'd be sending a car for me.
           Naturally, when Meadows turned up I thought he
           was one of your people.

HYDE: (*Nodding*) The other man – the one in the car –
           did you get a good look at him?

LARRY: No, I'm afraid I didn't.

*One of the Plain Clothes Men enters from the hall. HYDE
looks across at him, indicating the attaché case.*

127

HYDE: Harrison – take that down to the car, will you?

The MAN goes to the attaché case. He stares down at the contents in amazement.

HYDE: Well, go on. Anyone would think you'd never seen a case full of money before.

HARRISON: (*Simply*) I haven't, sir.

HYDE and LARRY exchange amused glances as HARRISON closes the lid and takes up the attaché case, moving to the door.

HYDE: Now – if you'd be good enough to come along with us, Mr Martin. (*With a faint smile*) I've got something I'd like to show you, for a change …

LARRY looks across at the INSPECTOR; puzzled.

CUT TO: The mews outside of LARRY MARTIN's flat. *The police car is parked outside of the entrance. EDDIE MEADOWS is seated in the back of the car with one of the PLAIN CLOTHES MEN. HARRISON comes out of the flat carrying the attaché case. He gets into the car sitting on the other side of MEADOWS who is scowling. LARRY and HYDE come out of the flat and get into the car which then moves off.*

CUT TO: INSPECTOR HYDE's Office at Scotland Yard. *HYDE is sitting behind a large mahogany desk, facing LARRY and LUTHER HARRIS. LUTHER appears worried and faintly puzzled by the INSPECTOR's manner.*

LUTHER: … But I've told you what happened. Andy gave me the ticket and asked me to go down to Victoria and pick up the case. After I left the hospital, I had second thoughts and decided I'd been a bit stupid – so I telephoned Larry and handed over the ticket.

HYDE: (*Rises*) And you didn't know what was in the case?

LUTHER: Of course I didn't! And I still don't believe there was four thousand pounds in it!

LARRY: It's true, Luther – there was.

HYDE: Nearly fifty thousand Deutsche Marks.

HYDE crosses to the light switch.

LUTHER: Well, where on earth did Phil get fifty thousand Deutsche Marks?

LARRY: We don't know. We don't even know whether the case belonged to Phil or not.

HYDE switches the lights on.

LUTHER: What d'you mean?

LARRY: Andy might have been lying – perhaps Phil never gave him the ticket in the first place.

LUTHER: Yes, that's possible, I suppose.

HYDE: Mr Harris – how often did Philip Martin and Andy Wilson visit your shop?

LUTHER: Oh – when they were on leave, several times a week.

HYDE: Did they ever meet anyone there – by appointment, I mean?

LUTHER: (*After a moment*) No, I don't think so.

HYDE: You don't think so?

LUTHER: Well, there was one occasion …

HYDE: Go on, Mr Harris.

LUTHER looks at the INSPECTOR, hesitates, then:

LUTHER: Several months ago a woman came into the shop and asked for a particular gramophone record. I only had one copy and it so happened Phil was in one of the cubicles listening to it. I told him the woman wanted to borrow the record but instead of handing it over he invited her into the cubicle.

129

	I was very annoyed at the time, but it worked out all right – she bought the record.
LARRY:	And you had the impression Phil had met this woman before?
LUTHER:	Oh, I don't know about that, but I had the feeling that … well, that he'd been expecting her.
HYDE:	What was she like, this woman – can you describe her?
LUTHER:	She was about forty-three or four – blonde – quite good looking. She wore a check suit with a diamond and ruby brooch on it …
LARRY:	Was the brooch like a basket of flowers – she wore it on her lapel?
LUTHER:	(*Surprised*) Yes, that's right.
LARRY:	(*To HYDE*) It sounds like the woman I told you about, the one I saw at Arundel – she was with Fletcher when he searched my flat.
HYDE:	(*To LUTHER*) Have you seen this woman since?

As HYDE speaks a PLAIN CLOTHES DETECTIVE SERGEANT enters the office. He carries several photographs.

LUTHER:	No, never …
HYDE:	Was Andy Wilson in the shop when this incident occurred?
LUTHER:	No, I don't think so. If I remember rightly, he turned up about half an hour later.

HYDE nods and looks at the SERGEANT.

| HYDE: | Are these the photographs? |
| SERGEANT: | Yes, sir. |

He hands the photographs to HYDE

| HYDE: | (*To LARRY*) This is what I wanted you to take a look at, Mr Martin. (*Rises from the desk*) These photographs were taken by Interpol – they arrived this morning. |

HYDE shows LARRY several of the photographs. They are of CLIFF FLETCHER, taken by an Interpol photographer.

HYDE: Do you know this man?

LARRY: Why yes – that's Fletcher!

HYDE: The man with the knife?

LARRY: That's right.

HYDE: You're sure it's Fletcher?

LARRY: I'm absolutely sure.

HYDE looks pleased that LARRY has identified FLETCHER. He hands LUTHER HARRIS one of the photographs.

HYDE: Do you happen to know this gentleman too, Mr Harris?

LUTHER studies the photograph for a moment, then looks up and shakes his head.

LUTHER: No.

HYDE: You've never seen him before?

LUTHER: No, I'm afraid I haven't.

HYDE: He's never patronised your establishment at any time?

LUTHER: (*Irritated*) If he had have done I'd have seen him, wouldn't I?

HYDE: (*Smiling*) Yes, I suppose you would, Mr Harris. (*To SERGEANT*) What about Meadows? Has he seen these photographs?

SERGEANT: Yes, sir. He made no comment, but I think he recognised him. Incidentally, Meadows says he knows nothing about this business, he was simply told to pick up Mr Martin, make sure he had the key. And take him down to the car.

HYDE: Do you believe that?

SERGEANT: Yes, I do, sir. You know Meadows, he hasn't got the guts to be mixed up in anything really big. Besides he had fifty pounds on him in cash – apparently that was the deal.

131

HYDE nods, then turns to LARRY and LUTHER HARRIS.

HYDE: (*Dismissing them*) Well, thank you, Mr Martin –
            Mr Harris …

LARRY: Inspector …

HYDE: Yes?

*LARRY indicates the photographs which the INSPECTOR is
holding.*

LARRY: Who is that man? Why are Interpol so interested
            in him?

HYDE: His real name is Sandman – Peter Sandman – but
            he works under many aliases. Fletcher happens
            to be one of them. The German police think he
            organised the Hamburg bank raid – you probably
            remember the one I mean, about eighteen months
            ago.

LARRY: No, I don't remember it.

HYDE: The manager was English, chap called Weston.
            He was murdered just as he came out of his
            office one night …

LARRY: No, I don't remember reading about it.

HYDE: It was in the papers. Your brother was stationed
            in Hamburg, wasn't he, sir?

*LARRY looks at the INSPECTOR. He realises what HYDE is
thinking.*

LARRY: Yes, he was …

CUT TO: *LARRY and LUTHER are in LARRY's car, driving
through the West End.*

LUTHER: … You know, I've been thinking, Larry. This is
            the third time I've been questioned by the police.

LARRY: The third time?

LUTHER: Yes. They came to my place the day after Phil
            died, and then Hyde dropped in the morning after
            I'd been to the hospital.

LARRY: Yes, well, I expect they've been checking up on all sorts of people.

LUTHER: I don't know about that. They certainly seem to be concentrating on me at the moment.

LARRY: Yes, well, obviously when I found the money I had to tell them about the ticket …

LUTHER: Yes, of course, Larry, I understand. I'm not blaming you, old man, it's just that – well … my shop wasn't the only place Phil and Andy visited, you know. They used to spend a devil of a lot of time at that coffee bar place.

LARRY: Which place was that?

LUTHER: Oh, I forget the name of it. It's on the King's Road … El Something-or-other … El Barbecue, I think it is.

LARRY: How do you know they spent a lot of time there?

LUTHER: (*Looking at LARRY*) I used to hear them talking about it. Besides, they took me there one night. It's a perfectly respectable place, Larry, I'm not suggesting there's anything funny about it. I'm just wondering if the police are as interested in it as they are in my place.

LARRY: It's not your shop they're interested in, Luther – it's you. After all, you were a pretty close friend of Phil's.

LUTHER: Yes, of course.

LARRY: (*After a moment*) Where shall I drop you?

LUTHER: Are you going near Cambridge Circus?

LARRY: Yes …

LUTHER: That'll do nicely. (*A moment, looking at LARRY*) Don't think I don't want to help you, Larry, but – well – anything to do with the police always seems to make me jittery.

LARRY: It's a guilty conscience.

LUTHER: (*Smiling*) Yes, I think it must be …

CUT TO: Outside the El Barbecue Coffee Bar in Chelsea. *LARRY is standing at the window, ostensibly looking at the menu hanging there. He glances around the interior of the coffee bar, his eyes finally resting on the counter.*

CUT TO: Inside the El Barbecue Coffee Bar which is a typical coffee bar in Chelsea.
Stools at the counter, an espresso machine, and sandwiches and pastries in glass cases.
The lighting is low and in one of the alcoves a young couple are gazing earnestly at one another over their coffee. Behind the bar, a middle-aged woman, JOYCE NAYLOR, is making sandwiches. She has had a long day and looks tired and irritable. OSCAR NAYLOR – her husband – a tough, bald-headed man of about fifty, is at the till. He moves to a customer at the counter giving him his change. The man nods and moves to the door. LARRY enters, holding the door open for the man who has just left the counter. He closes the door and goes to the counter, sitting on one of the stools.
LARRY: Coffee, please.
OSCAR nods and moves to the machine. JOYCE puts the sandwiches she has just made into the glass case. LARRY looks discreetly from one to the other as he lights a cigarette.
LARRY: You're not very busy tonight.
JOYCE shrugs. She is obviously too tired to make conversation. OSCAR answers for her.
OSCAR: Slacks off a bit about this time. Picks up again around half-nine to ten.
He brings the coffee to LARRY.
LARRY: Thanks. (*He stirs the coffee*) Have you been here long?
OSCAR is surprised by the question.

OSCAR:	What – me?
LARRY:	Yes.
OSCAR:	About four years.
LARRY:	I wonder if you could help me. My name's Martin – Larry Martin.

JOYCE gives OSCAR a look, obviously recognising LARRY's name.

LARRY:	(*Noticing the look*) Perhaps you've heard of me?
JOYCE:	Yes, I've heard of you – you're a photographer. It was your brother that … (*She hesitates*)
LARRY:	That's right.
OSCAR:	(*Quietly looking at LARRY*) What is it you want, Mr Martin?
LARRY:	Well, I'm making certain inquiries about Phil, my brother, and I thought perhaps you might be able to help me. I understand that Phil, and a friend of his called Andy Wilson, used to come here quite a lot.
OSCAR:	Yes, they did – but I didn't have much to do with them, I'm afraid.
JOYCE:	That was when Joseph was here …
LARRY:	Joseph?
OSCAR:	He was a waiter, he used to work here. He was friendly with your brother and that other chap – what was his name?
LARRY:	Andy Wilson …
OSCAR:	That's right. They were always fooling about. Pulling each other's leg – that sort of thing. In the end I got a bit fed up with it.

A customer arrives at the bar and OSCAR nods to JOYCE to take care of him. JOYCE moves, somewhat reluctantly, away from LARRY and OSCAR.

LARRY:	You say my brother was friendly with this man – Joseph?
OSCAR:	Yes.
LARRY:	How friendly?
OSCAR:	I don't know.
LARRY:	Did they meet – I mean, apart from here?
OSCAR:	I've told you, I don't know. If I was you, I'd have a word with Joseph. (*He looks at his wristwatch*) He'll be here in about fifteen minutes.
LARRY:	(*Surprised*) I thought you said he'd left you?
OSCAR:	He has – but he pops in for a free coffee every night. He's working at a pub on the Brompton Road. (*He nods towards one of the alcoves*) Take a pew. I'll let you know when he gets here.

LARRY looks at OSCAR, hesitates, then with a little nod he picks up his cup of coffee and crosses over to one of the alcoves. OSCAR watches him, casually cleaning the top of the bar counter. As he does so, after a moment he glances across at JOYCE and goes behind the curtain which separates the bar from the kitchen. There is a telephone on the wall at the entrance to the kitchen. OSCAR removes the receiver and starts to dial a number.

CUT TO: Inside the El Barbecue. As before.

LARRY is sitting at the table in the alcove. He is just finishing his second cup of coffee. The ashtray is half full of cigarette ends. He glances across at the bar – a waitress has taken over and there is no sign of OSCAR and JOYCE. LARRY is about to light another cigarette when he realises that someone has slipped into the seat opposite him. It is CLARE SELDON. LARRY slowly lowers his lighter and tries to conceal his astonishment.

CLARE: Good evening …

LARRY rises to his feet.

LARRY: You wouldn't be Joseph, by any chance?

CLARE: (*Tensely shaking her head*) Mr Martin, please
              sit down. I've got to talk to you – it's
              important.

LARRY hesitates, then sits down. He nods towards the bar.

LARRY: Did <u>he</u> send for you?

CLARE: Yes. Look, Mr Martin – I haven't got much
              time. I've got an appointment at eight o'clock
              and I've got to keep it.

LARRY: With our knife-throwing friend, Mr Fletcher?

CLARE: I didn't know what was going to happen that
              afternoon – I didn't know they were going to
              murder Quayle, honestly I didn't …

LARRY: What did you think they were going to do?

CLARE: I didn't know. I thought perhaps they were
              going to abduct him and … (*Shaking her
              head*) I didn't come here to discuss Quayle. I
              … (*Hesitates*)

LARRY: Go on, Mrs Seldon.

CLARE: I want to talk to you about Phil … about your
              brother …

*LARRY looks at her, trying to make up his mind whether she
is serious or just putting on an act for his benefit.*

CLARE: Ever since your brother died you've been
              making enquiries about him. You've been
              trying to find out why he went to
              Maidenhead, why he was interested in that
              book.

LARRY: Well?

CLARE: (*Leaning towards LARRY across the table*) I
              can tell you why he went to Maidenhead, Mr
              Martin. I can tell you about the book, I can

	tell you everything you want to know if ... (*She hesitates again*)
LARRY:	If what?

There is a slight pause.

CLARE:	(*A shade embarrassed*) If I'm going to help you, you've got to help me. That's only fair, isn't it?
LARRY:	(*With just a faint trace of sarcasm*) Yes, that's only fair, Mrs Seldon. (*After a tiny pause*) What is it you want me to do?
CLARE:	I don't want you to do anything, but ... you've got something I want. If you'll give it to me – now – tonight – I'll tell you about Phil.
LARRY:	(*Puzzled*) What is it I've got that could possibly ... (*A sudden realisation*) Oh – the key ...
CLARE:	The key? (*Shaking her head*) No – no, I'm not talking about the key, I'm talking about the parcel, Mr Martin.
LARRY:	What parcel?
CLARE:	A parcel was sent to your brother from Germany – it was addressed to Phil and sent to your flat.
LARRY:	(*Shaking his head*) I know nothing about this.
CLARE:	It hasn't arrived yet?
LARRY:	No ...
CLARE:	You're sure?
LARRY:	Of course I'm sure! If it had arrived, I should have handed it over to the police.
CLARE:	Yes, well, don't, Mr Martin.

She rises and takes a card out of her handbag.

CLARE:	Not if you really want to know the truth about your brother. When the parcel arrives ring me

at this number. (*She gives LARRY the card*)
You won't regret it, Mr Martin, I promise
you.

CLARE leaves the table. LARRY watches her, then slowly looks down at the telephone number on the card.

CUT TO: Outside the front door of LARRY MARTIN's flat. *DOUGLAS TALBOT arrives. He is carrying a briefcase. He pauses for a moment, looking towards LARRY's front door. He moves to the door and rings the bell. A pause. He rings the bell a second time. He looks rather impatient and is about to ring the bell for a third time when the door opens. LARRY is standing there. He has taken off his jacket and loosened his tie. He looks surprised on seeing TALBOT.*

TALBOT: Good evening, Mr Martin.

LARRY: (*Flatly*) Good evening.

LARRY was obviously enjoying a moment's well-earned relaxation and he is irritated by this surprise visit, especially as he does not like TALBOT.

TALBOT: I'm sorry to – er – drop in on you like this, I
            suppose I should have given you a ring …

LARRY: (*Curtly*) You wouldn't have got me any way.
            I've been out most of the evening.

TALBOT: Oh – well, in that case …

LARRY: Won't you come in?

TALBOT: Thank you.

TALBOT enters LARRY's flat and LARRY closes the door. He indicates the living room and TALBOT smiles and goes in. LARRY looks after him for a moment before following him. In spite of his irritation at DOUGLAS TALBOT's visit he is curious about the purpose of it. TALBOT stands in the centre of the room. Glancing discreetly about him as LARRY enters.

LARRY: What can I do for you?

TALBOT looks at LARRY and then opens his briefcase. He takes out a brown paper parcel from the case and hands it to LARRY.

TALBOT: This parcel arrived at the hotel this morning. It's addressed to your brother, so Mrs Curtis asked me to deliver it to you.

LARRY: That's very kind of her. I hope you haven't made a special journey?

TALBOT: No, of course not. I had an appointment in town. Incidentally, I wonder if you would be kind enough to sign this slip?

He produces a pen and a receipt book

LARRY: Slip?

TALBOT: It's a receipt for the parcel.

LARRY: Yes … certainly.

LARRY signs the receipt and hands it back to TALBOT.

TALBOT: In my opinion the parcel ought to have been handed over to the police … but Mrs Curtis thought otherwise.

LARRY: I thought you and Mrs Curtis usually saw eye to eye about things?

TALBOT: We do as a rule but … (*He shrugs*)

LARRY looks at the parcel again, putting it down on the table in front of him.

LARRY: I see it was posted in Germany.

TALBOT: Apparently.

He closes his briefcase and moves towards the hall.

TALBOT: Now, if you'll excuse me …

LARRY nods. TALBOT crosses towards the front door, followed by LARRY.

LARRY: Is there any news?

TALBOT: (*Turning; faintly surprised*) News?

LARRY: About the Quayle murder? Are there any developments?

TALBOT: Oh, I see what you mean. No, I don't think so. The police have been to the hotel several times, of course, and questioned Vanessa … Mrs Curtis … but they don't seem to be getting very far. Incidentally, Martin, I understand you told the Inspector that Quayle dropped in on you one day and asked for that key.

LARRY: Yes, I did.

TALBOT: Well, I can't imagine why Thomas should do that.

LARRY: Well, he did … I assure you.

TALBOT: He knew perfectly well it belonged to his sister. It's the key to her private suite, you know.

LARRY: Yes, so the Inspector told me.

TALBOT: (*Shaking his head*) I just can't imagine why Thomas should want that key.

LARRY: (*Quite simply*) Perhaps he wanted to open the door, Mr Talbot.

TALBOT looks at LARRY, not quite sure how to take this remark. LARRY opens the front door.

LARRY: Good night.

TALBOT hesitates, then with a curt nod he goes out. LARRY closes the door. He goes back into the living room, crosses to the table and picks up the parcel. He tears off the brown paper wrapping, revealing cardboard wrapping secured by a rubber band. Slowly he removes the band and the cardboard. He stares down at the uncovered object. It is a copy of the book of poems by Hilaire Belloc. LARRY glances through the pages of the book. His attention is suddenly arrested by some pencilled words on the fly leaf of the book. They are in German. Beneath the words is the name "Linderhof". LARRY stares down in puzzled silence at the book. After a moment he closes the book and puts his hand in his pocket. He takes out the card given to him by CLARE SELDON. He

141

looks at the card, makes a decision, and crosses to the telephone. He puts down the book of poems near the telephone and takes up the receiver. He hesitates, wondering if he is doing the right thing. He looks at the card and dials the number. After a little while we hear the number ringing out at the other end. The receiver is lifted and we hear CLARE SELDON's voice.

CLARE's VOICE: Hello? ... Mrs Seldon speaking.

LARRY: This is Larry Martin. I thought I'd let you know the parcel's just arrived.

CLARE's VOICE: I see. Well, Mr Martin, now it's up to you.

LARRY: What do you mean?

CLARE's VOICE: Do you want to meet me, or don't you?

LARRY looks down at the book, hesitates, then:

LARRY: If I didn't want to meet you I wouldn't be phoning you, would I?

CLARE's VOICE: You might ... if you'd been in touch with the police.

LARRY: (*Emphatically*) I haven't been in touch with the police.

CLARE's VOICE: Very well. (*Briskly*) Do you know Blackgate Common?

LARRY: Yes ...

CLARE's VOICE: On the north side of the Common there's an old horse trough ... about thirty yards away there's a lane leading down to a farm. I'll park my car about half-way down the lane. It's fifty yards or so off the main road.

LARRY: But why Blackgate? Why can't we meet in town?

CLARE's VOICE: (*Curtly*) Because I shan't be in town, Mr Martin. I'll see you there in about an hour.

LARRY: Yes, all right.

142

There is a click as CLARE replaces the receiver at the other end. Slowly, LARRY replaces his own receiver and takes up the book. He looks at it thoughtfully for a moment, then crosses to the chair taking up his jacket. He puts the book in the pocket of the jacket, then puts the jacket on as he goes out into the hall.

CUT TO: Outside the front door of LARRY MARTIN's flat. *RUTH comes up the stairs, moving to the front door. She opens her handbag, looking for her key. The front door opens and LARRY comes out, closing the door behind him. He is surprised to see RUTH standing there.*

LARRY: Hello, Ruth! What are you doing here?

RUTH: I said I'd be coming back, remember? The Delton Agency are expecting those prints tomorrow …

LARRY: Oh yes, of course.

RUTH: What happened about Fletcher? Was he the man they arrested?

LARRY: They didn't arrest anyone.

RUTH stares at him.

LARRY: I'll tell you all about it when I get back … if you're still here.

RUTH: I'll be here all right, I've bags of work to do.

LARRY is just about to dash off when a sudden thought occurs to him. He takes the book out of his jacket pocket.

LARRY: Just a minute … you read German, don't you, Ruth?

RUTH: A little … yes. Why?

RUTH watches him as he opens the book and indicates the writing on the fly leaf.

LARRY: What does that say?

RUTH looks at the page in the book, reading the words to herself.

143

RUTH: (*Slowly; translating*) "This is … the book … you
          need … Linderhof".

*LARRY nods and returns the book to his pocket. RUTH is
obviously puzzled.*

RUTH: Is that the book Phil was reading? The book that
          Andy Wilson …

LARRY pats her on the arm.

LARRY: I'll tell you all about it later, darling.

*He dashes off, down the staircase. RUTH stares after him,
puzzled and bewildered, then she starts to search for her door
key again. Suddenly she looks up, remembering what LARRY
has said.*

RUTH: (*To herself; with a quizzical smile*) Darling …

*RUTH takes the key from her handbag, puts it in the door and
turns the lock. As she does so we notice the lucky charm
bracelet she wears on her wrist.*

CUT TO: Blackgate Common. Night.

*LARRY's car pulls into the side of the road. LARRY gets out.
He is carrying a large torch. He stands there peering at
something a little distance away. He walks towards the object.
It is a horse trough. He looks down at it, then looks
thoughtfully into the blackness beyond, his mind dwelling on
CLARE SELDON's instructions. He walks to the entrance to
the lane described by MRS SELDON and looks down the lane.
He turns suddenly as if hearing something behind him. It is
nothing; he is just a little on edge. He goes down the lane,
bordered on either side with bushes and shrubbery. LARRY
approaches a turning in the lane. He stops and stares ahead.
He remains there for a moment. He has seen a small car
parked at the side of the lane. He moves to the driving seat
window of the car and sees that the car is unoccupied.
LARRY shines his torch into the car. It is empty. He switches
off the torch and glances up and down the lane. He is puzzled*

144

– not quite sure what to do now. He puts the torch in his overcoat pocket and lights a cigarette. He inhales thoughtfully, looking down the lane. He decides to continue on down the lane. As he moves forward, he trips on a pothole in the ground. He swears under his breath and takes out his torch again, shining it in front of him as he goes forward. Suddenly, he stops dead. He stares down at the ground. He sees a woman's leg protruding from one of the bushes. After a moment, he bends down, parting the bushes. He reacts with horror as he reveals the body of a woman. She has been strangled. Slowly, LARRY reaches out and gently turns the body so that we see the woman's face – it is CLARE SELDON. As he stands looking at CLARE there is the sound of cars approaching on the main road.

CUT TO: Blackgate Common.
Two police cars drive up to the horse trough. INSPECTOR HYDE gets out of one of them, followed by the SERGEANT, and several policemen get out of the other car. HYDE indicates that they follow him, and they move towards the entrance to the winding lane.

CUT TO: Blackgate Common.
LARRY has now risen to his feet. He is still looking down at the body. Slowly he averts his eyes. He turns as he hears footsteps in the distance. He walks slowly towards the parked car. As he reaches it, HYDE quickly comes from the opposite direction, followed by the SERGEANT and the POLICE CONSTABLES.
HYDE: (*Urgently*) Martin … Are you all right?
LARRY stares at him for a second, then turns, indicating the body of CLARE SELDON. HYDE and the others move towards the body. LARRY looks after them. He presses a hand to his eyes and leans weakly against the car.

145

CUT TO: Blackgate Common.

LARRY and HYDE are standing beside CLARE's car. An ambulance goes past them down the lane. They watch it, then LARRY continues speaking to HYDE.

LARRY: ... So after Talbot left I phoned Clare Seldon and arranged to meet her here.

HYDE: Not exactly an ideal meeting place ... especially at this time of night.

LARRY: No, but she insisted on meeting here. I wanted to see her in town, but she wouldn't hear of it.

HYDE: I see. (*After a moment*) This coffee bar you mentioned ... what was the name of it again?

LARRY: "El Barbecue". It's just off the King's Road ...

HYDE: (*Nods*) And when you got back to your flat after visiting the coffee bar, this Talbot character turned up with the parcel ... this book?

LARRY: Yes, but he didn't know it was a book ... at least, he didn't appear to know. He just said it was a parcel that had arrived at the hotel ... the Falcon, that's it ... for my brother.

HYDE: When did it arrive ... did he say?

LARRY: I think he said this morning. Anyway, Mrs Curtis asked Talbot to drop it in as he was coming up to town.

HYDE: H'm.

LARRY: Now, may I ask a question Inspector?

HYDE: (*Smiling faintly*) What brought us here? We had a phone call from a woman. She told us you were coming here. (*Looking at LARRY*) She said you were going to be murdered.

LARRY: Who was this woman?

HYDE: (*Shrugs*) I don't know ... she didn't give her name. Have you any idea who it was, Mr Martin?

146

LARRY: (*Puzzled; shaking his head*) Why, no … no, I
haven't …

CUT TO: The mews where LARRY MARTIN's flat is.
*LARRY is closing the doors to his garage, having just parked
his car inside. He locks the doors and moves to the flat
entrance and goes in.*

CUT TO: Outside LARRY MARTIN's front door.
*LARRY comes up the stairs. He looks tired and thoughtful.
He is on the point of putting his key in the lock when
something attracts his attention. He looks down with a
puzzled air. He stoops and picks something up. It is a
woman's shoe. He stares at it for a moment, recognising it as
RUTH's shoe. He quickly unlocks the door and goes in.*

CUT TO: The hall and living room of LARRY MARTIN's
flat.
*LARRY closes the front door and moves quickly to the living
room.*
LARRY: (*Calling as he goes*) Ruth! Are you here?
He stops dead. The room is empty.
LARRY: (*Calling*) Ruth!
*He goes quickly to the studio door, opening it and looking
inside. He switches the light on and off, then moves back to
the centre of the living room. He sees that RUTH's chair has
been over-turned and that some papers are on the floor. He is
moving towards them when he sees something on the floor.
He picks it up. It is RUTH's charm bracelet.*

END OF EPISODE FIVE

EPISODE SIX

OPEN TO: The hall and living room of LARRY MARTIN's flat.

LARRY hurries into the living room from the hall. He is carrying the shoe.

LARRY: (*Calling*) Ruth! Are you here? … Ruth!

He goes quickly to the studio door, opening it and looking inside. He switches the light on and off, then moves back to the centre of the living room. He sees that RUTH's chair has been over-turned and that some papers are on the floor. He is moving towards them when he sees something on the floor. He picks it up. It is RUTH's charm bracelet. He is puzzled and worried. He makes as though to pick up the telephone when the doorbell rings. He leaves the shoe and the bracelet on the desk and hurries to the door. He opens it. CLIFF FLETCHER is standing in the doorway. He is wearing a double-breasted raincoat.

FLETCHER: (*With sarcasm*) Still looking for your secretary, Mr Martin?

LARRY suddenly recognises FLETCHER and, losing his temper, grabs him by the lapels and pulls him into the hall.

LARRY: Where is Ruth? What the hell have you done with her?

FLETCHER, taken by surprise, slowly releases himself.

FLETCHER: Take it easy, Mr Martin. Take it easy. (*He straightens his coat*)

LARRY stares at FLETCHER for a moment, then he slowly closes the front door. FLETCHER gives LARRY a little smile and strolls into the living room. LARRY follows him.

LARRY: (*Quietly*) Get to the point. What is it you want?

FLETCHER: You're worried about Miss Sanders, aren't you, Martin? There's no need to be – not if you're sensible.

LARRY: (*Controlling himself*) Where is Ruth? What have you done with her?

151

FLETCHER: She's in a flat on the other side of Town. Don't worry, she's all right. The moment you give the word – (*He nods towards the telephone*) I'll tell my friends to release her.

LARRY: What word? What are you talking about?

FLETCHER sits on the arm of the settee.

FLETCHER: Mr Martin, I don't want to play this rough, not if I can help it. I want things to be nice and friendly between us. I've got a proposition to put to you …

LARRY: What is your proposition?

FLETCHER: You've got a key; it's a copy of the one you gave the Inspector – the one that belongs to Mrs Curtis.

LARRY: Well?

FLETCHER: Give me that key and I'll release Miss Sanders.

LARRY shakes his head.

FLETCHER: You refuse?

LARRY: When I know Ruth's all right – when I know she's free – you can have the key.

FLETCHER looks at LARRY for a moment, then crosses to the telephone. He dials a number; as the number rings out he stands watching LARRY. The receiver is lifted at the other end and a man's voice can be heard. We cannot hear what the man is saying.

FLETCHER: (*On phone*) … This is Cliff … Release the girl … (*Annoyed*) Don't argue, do as I tell you! … (*Suddenly*) Wait a minute! Tell her to phone Martin from a call box … He's waiting for the call …

FLETCHER replaces the receiver and looks at LARRY again.

FLETCHER: Now get me the key.

LARRY hesitates, then crosses towards his desk.

152

CUT TO: The hall and living room of LARRY MARTIN's flat. As before.

The telephone on LARRY's desk is ringing. LARRY snatches up the receiver. FLETCHER stands watching him.

LARRY: (*On the phone, tensely*) … Is that you, Ruth? … Are you all right? … Is there anyone with you? … Are you sure, Ruth? … Where's the phone box? … (*Relieved*) Get back into the cab and come straight back here … (*He replaces the receiver*)

FLETCHER: Well, Mr Martin – satisfied?

LARRY doesn't answer.

FLETCHER: I'm not interested in your secretary, I'm interested in that key. Now I've kept my part of the bargain, you keep yours.

LARRY hesitates, then takes the key out of his pocket and gives it to FLETCHER. FLETCHER quickly examines it. After a moment he looks at LARRY again.

FLETCHER: … Are you sure this is the one – the one you had made – the copy of Mrs Curtis's?

LARRY: Yes, of course I'm sure! …

FLETCHER continues to stare at him, then a moment of annoyance and disappointment crosses his face and with an angry gesture he tosses the key onto the floor and goes out into the hall. LARRY stands, staring towards the hall. Puzzled by FLETCHER's behaviour. We hear the front door close.

CUT TO: The hall and living room of LARRY MARTIN's flat.

RUTH is curled up on the settee, drinking a cup of coffee. She looks tired and a shade tense. LARRY and the INSPECTOR sit facing her. HYDE is holding the key in his hand and is talking to LARRY about it.

HYDE: ... I still don't see why Fletcher threw away the key – not after going to such lengths to get hold of it.

LARRY: Neither do I, Inspector.

RUTH: Perhaps he thought you were going to give him the original one?

LARRY: No, he knew I hadn't got the original. In any case, this is an exact copy.

RUTH: (*Thoughtfully*) I wonder, Larry ...

LARRY: What do you mean?

RUTH: I have a feeling this key isn't an exact copy, and that Fletcher spotted the difference.

HYDE: Mr Martin, I think she's right!

HYDE looks at the key and then suddenly looks up.

HYDE: There's no number on this. Was there a number on the other one?

LARRY takes the key from the INSPECTOR and examines it.

LARRY: (*Quietly, thoughtfully*) Yes – I believe there was ...

HYDE: (*Nodding*) That's what Fletcher was looking for. He wasn't interested in the key – he was looking for the number. (*A sudden thought*) Wait a minute! I wonder if this ties up with the photographs.

LARRY: The photographs?

HYDE: I sent the Stansdale photographs down to our Code people. They seemed to think that the photographs were part of a code ...

RUTH: And you think the number on the key ...

HYDE: (*Interrupting her*) I think the number is the second half of the code, the part we're now looking for.

LARRY: I'm not sure I understand this, Inspector.

HYDE: Mrs Stansdale was photographed holding an accordion – her fingers on the keyboard.

LARRY nods.

HYDE: Each photograph was the same, except for the position of her fingers. It's my bet the various photographs, plus the number on the key, represents the complete code.

HYDE looks at LARRY, hesitates, then:

HYDE: Mr Martin, I wonder if you would do something for me?

LARRY: Yes, of course, Inspector – what is it?

HYDE: (*Thoughtfully*) I feel sure Andy Wilson knows all about this. (*Facing LARRY*) I'd like you to have another talk with him, Mr Martin.

CUT TO: A hospital convalescent ward.

ANDY WILSON is sitting in an armchair, reading a book. He wears pyjamas and a dressing gown and looks considerably fitter than the last time we saw him. He looks up on hearing someone approaching. He looks a shade uneasy as LARRY reaches the armchair. LARRY carries several magazines in his hand.

LARRY: Hello, Andy! How are you feeling?

ANDY: Oh, I'm all right – thanks.

LARRY: Good. They tell me you should be out of here by the end of next week.

ANDY: (*Trying to conceal his anxiety*) Yes …

LARRY: You don't look too pleased about it …

ANDY doesn't reply.

LARRY: Oh, I brought you these.

LARRY puts the magazines down on a small table and indicates a vacant chair.

LARRY: Do you mind if I sit down?

ANDY: Go ahead …

LARRY: (*Casually; sitting in the chair*) Well, I suppose you've heard the news?

ANDY: What news?

155

LARRY: They picked up Fletcher last night. He broke
            down – told them the whole story … (*Casually,
            turning over the pages of one of the magazines*)
            It's funny, isn't it? You wouldn't think a tough
            type like Fletcher would break down and …

ANDY: Look, Larry – what the hell are you talking
            about? Who's Fletcher? I've never heard of him
            …

LARRY: (*Glancing down at the magazine again*) No?
            Well, he's heard of you. (*He looks up, leans
            forward and puts his hand on Andy's knee*)
            Andy, when you get out of here, you're going to
            need help – every possible help you can get.
            Financial and otherwise.

ANDY looks up at LARRY.

LARRY: If you help me, Andy, I'll stand by you – if you
            don't, you're on your own.

ANDY hesitates.

ANDY: What is it you want to know?

LARRY: When did you first meet Fletcher?

*ANDY hesitates again, then suddenly makes up his mind to
talk.*

ANDY: I used to know him years ago – before I joined
            the Army. Then I met him in London one night,
            when I was on leave. Your brother was with me.
            We had a few drinks and then Fletcher took us to
            a club just off Ralston Square. It was one of
            those new, lush, chi-chi places. Phil and I had
            never been in a place like that before and it was a
            bit of a lark – at first, at any rate. Fletcher
            showed us how to play baccarat and between us
            we won the best part of eighty quid. We were
            tickled pink, of course – very pleased with
            ourselves. We went back to the club the next

	night and the night after that … (*A shrug*) You can guess what happened.
LARRY:	How much did you lose?
ANDY:	Between us – nearly six hundred pounds.
LARRY:	But where did you get the money from?
ANDY:	From Fletcher – he lent us the money and we gave him I.O.U.s …
LARRY:	(*Quietly*) Go on, Andy …
ANDY:	At first Fletcher appeared to be indifferent about the whole business – then one night he met Phil and me in a coffee bar and told us that he'd just found out that we were friendly with a man called David Weston. He hadn't just found out about Weston, of course, he'd known for weeks that the three of us were friends. Weston was the manager of the National Bank in Hamburg. Phil and I met him the first week we arrived in Germany. Fletcher told us that Weston had information about the transfer of large sums of money to the Brunderschaft Engineering Works at Dusseldorf. He told us if we got that information for him, he'd return the I.O.U.s …
LARRY:	Go on …
ANDY:	He said he and his friends intended to rob the bank and if all went well Phil and I would get a cut as well as the I.O.U.s. You know what happened. They did the job all right and then flew the money to England.
LARRY:	But you didn't get paid?
ANDY:	(*Shaking his head*) No. It was all laid on for us to get paid – that's why Phil went to the Falcon Hotel. It was understood that if Phil received a copy of a certain book everything was going

according to plan and he'd be handed the I.O.U.s and the money.

LARRY: Who was going to hand over the money – Fletcher?

ANDY: No, someone else – someone neither of us had met. That's why Phil had to have the book, to identify himself. And that's why I took it after Phil was murdered, I thought the book might incriminate him …

LARRY: I see. Go on, Andy …

ANDY: Phil telephoned me one morning from Maidenhead. He said he was worried. Although he'd got the book it didn't look as if our cut was coming. He said the manager of the hotel – Douglas Talbot – had contacted him and was going to report back. Later Talbot told Phil there were certain difficulties about the share-out. Phil didn't trust him. He thought he was trying to pull a fast one and he warned him if he didn't stump up he'd go to the police. Talbot gave Phil a smooth line and said everything would be all right. Well, it wasn't all right. The bastard dropped in on Phil later that night and you know the rest.

LARRY: So it was Talbot who murdered Phil?

ANDY nods.

LARRY: Was it Talbot who tried to kill you?

ANDY: Yes, he knew Phil had spoken to me about him and he thought I might go to the police.

LARRY: I see.

ANDY: I think Talbot was telling Phil the truth. Most of the money was hidden by another member of the gang – a chap called Quayle. Quayle refused to divulge the whereabouts of the money but in case of accidents devised a code.

LARRY: (*Quietly*) Yes, we know about the code.

ANDY: (*Looking at LARRY*) Did Fletcher tell you about it?

LARRY: (*Hesitantly*) No …

ANDY is curious and puzzled by LARRY's manner.

ANDY: What happened with Cliff? How did the police pick him up?

LARRY hesitates and then rises – he looks down at ANDY.

LARRY: I'm afraid I lied to you. The police haven't arrested Fletcher.

ANDY: (*Stares at LARRY in amazement*) They haven't?

LARRY: No, but don't worry – they will …

LARRY is gone before ANDY can reply. ANDY glares angrily after him.

CUT TO: INSPECTOR HYDE's Office at Scotland Yard.

It is a well-furnished office with a large window looking down on the Embankment.

HYDE is sitting behind his desk, facing LARRY.

HYDE: … So Andy Wilson thought we'd got Fletcher and decided to talk?

LARRY: Yes. Whether he was telling the truth or not it's difficult to say; but one thing I'm sure about – he was telling the truth about Talbot.

HYDE: You think Talbot murdered your brother?

LARRY: Yes, I do.

HYDE: And you think he's the one behind all this – you think he's running this show?

LARRY: I don't know.

He rises and crosses to the window.

LARRY: It could be Talbot, I suppose – it could be one
              of many people.
HYDE: I think originally the man behind all this was
              Quayle; that's why Fletcher murdered him.
              It's the old story, Martin – when thieves fall
              out …

HYDE rises and joins LARRY at the window.

HYDE: I saw Mrs Curtis this morning and got details
              of the key. Major Osborne, our code expert, is
              working on it – together with the
              photographs. (*A shrug*) Whether we shall be
              lucky and find the money remains to be seen.

*There is a knock on the door and a PLAIN-CLOTHES
DETECTIVE-SERGEANT enters.*

SERGEANT: Excuse me, sir.
HYDE: (*Turning*) Yes, Sergeant – what is it?
SERGEANT: Major Osborne's just telephoned through, sir.
              They're still having difficulty with the code
              …
HYDE: I bet they are …
SERGEANT: They seem to think it may have something to
              do with Venice, sir …
HYDE: Venice?
SERGEANT: Yes – does that make sense to you, sir?
HYDE: No, it certainly doesn't! (*Irritated*) Venice for
              God's sake! Osborne's obviously on the
              wrong track – he's just wasting his time.
LARRY: Wait a minute! I'm not so sure … (*To
              SERGEANT*) The number on the key plus the
              photographs produced a code, and the code …
SERGEANT: … Appears to have something to do with
              Venice. (*Nodding*) Yes, sir.

LARRY looks puzzled, thoughtful.

HYDE: What are you thinking about, Martin?

LARRY: (*After a moment*) I was just thinking …
HYDE: (*Exasperated*) Yes, I know – but what about!
LARRY: (*Thoughtfully*) There was a chest in Quayle's
              antique shop. The top part of it – the lid – was
              made out of a picture – a Canaletto print …
              The chest was marked sold but I remember
              looking at it and thinking …
SERGEANT: (*Interrupting him*) What was the picture of,
              sir?
LARRY: It was a picture of Venice … St Mark's
              Square …

HYDE moves down to LARRY.

HYDE: Are you sure about this?
LARRY: Yes, I'm positive.
HYDE: (*To SERGEANT, briskly*) Tell Osborne I want
              to see him, and get me Arundel on the phone.
              I want to talk to Inspector Lang straight away,
              it's urgent.

*The SERGEANT goes out. LARRY looks at HYDE as the
INSPECTOR returns to his desk.*

LARRY: (*Puzzled*) But there can't be anything at
              Quayle's place. The Arundel police must
              have searched it from top to bottom.

The telephone rings.

HYDE: They can search it again! (*Picks up the
              receiver*) … Yes, speaking … Where did you
              say it was from – Maidenhead? Put him
              through …

He looks across at LARRY.

HYDE: Hello, Sergeant – what's the trouble? … I see
              … Yes, I understand … When did it happen?
              … Who identified the body? … M'm … No,
              don't do that, I'll come down straight away
              … Thanks for phoning …

161

HYDE rises, replacing the receiver and turns towards LARRY again.

HYDE: You can cross Mr Talbot off your list.

He gets his hat and coat and opens the door.

HYDE: Someone battered his face in and dumped his body in a ditch two hundred yards from the hotel …

CUT TO: A quiet country lane near Maidenhead.

The lane is full of police officials and local journalists. There is the body of a dead man in a nearby ditch. Police photographers are still taking pictures of the murdered man. A farm labourer discovered the body and this man now stands amongst a group of onlookers, describing his experience. HYDE and a local detective, SERGEANT WAINWRIGHT – stand near the ditch. HYDE is listening to what WAINWRIGHT is saying, at the same time casually glancing at a diary which has been taken from the dead man's jacket. A police ambulance is in the background.

WAINWRIGHT: It's a good job Mrs Curtis identified him, sir, because we hadn't a clue as to who he was … He must have taken a hell of a beating, poor devil.

HYDE: Yes, I could see that … Where is Mrs Curtis now?

WAINWRIGHT: She went back to the hotel about an hour ago.

HYDE: When did she last see Talbot?

WAINWRIGHT: Apparently, he left the hotel this morning; he has an appointment with a man called Fletcher.

HYDE looks at WAINWRIGHT.

WAINWRIGHT: She wasn't expecting him back until this evening.

HYDE gets in the back of a police car

WAINWRIGHT: Mrs Curtis is in quite a state, sir. I doubt whether you'll get much sense out of her.

HYDE: (*Drily*) I'll do my best, Sergeant.

HYDE shuts the door of the car and it drives off.

CUT TO: VANESSA CURTIS's room at the Royal Falcon Hotel.

VANESSA CURTIS is sitting in an armchair. She is smoking a cigarette and looks tense and distinctly "on edge". The INSPECTOR stands near the fireplace, looking down at her.

HYDE: … I'm sorry, Mrs Curtis, but I don't think you've been perfectly frank with me about Talbot.

VANESSA: I've told you all I know, I can't tell you more than that.

HYDE: You say he had an appointment with a man called Fletcher?

VANESSA: (*Tensely*) I think he had an appointment with someone called Fletcher. He didn't mention the appointment – it was just that I overheard a telephone conversation.

HYDE: I see. Mrs Curtis, after the death of Philip Martin I made certain enquiries about you – about Mr Talbot – and about this hotel.

VANESSA: Well?

HYDE: Before your husband died Talbot used to be an accountant – he had a small business of his own. Suddenly, on your husband's death he moved down to Maidenhead and took over the running of this hotel.

VANESSA: No, that's not true, Inspector – that's not what happened. Douglas … Talbot … was staying here when my husband was killed in

163

a railway accident. Naturally I was distressed and confused … It happened so quickly – I – I just didn't know which way to turn …

HYDE: Yes, I can imagine that …

VANESSA: Talbot started by being helpful, then before I knew what was happening, he'd gained complete control of my affairs. (*Emotionally, turning away from HYDE*) He was a dreadful person; he had a strange influence over certain people …

HYDE: (*Quietly*) Over you, Mrs Curtis?

VANESSA: (*Nodding*) Yes … it was Talbot who murdered Philip Martin … Martin was going back to town that night, but Talbot made me go to his room and talk to him. He was obviously frightened that Martin might go to the police about something or other …

HYDE: I see. (*After a moment*) Mrs Curtis, tell me – was Talbot a friend of your brother's?

VANESSA: No, Thomas hated him – but curiously enough I think they were in some kind of business together. I never did discover what it was …

HYDE takes the diary out of his pocket.

HYDE: We found this diary on Talbot. There are several phone numbers in it.

The INSPECTOR opens the diary and then hands it to VANESSA. She looks at it.

VANESSA: The first two are shops in Maidenhead – tradespeople – I don't know the others … (*Looking at the diary again*) Wait a minute … Court 7214 … that's a number he was always ringing.

HYDE: Who is it – do you know?

VANESSA: It's a shop in London; it belongs to a friend of
           Talbot's. A man called Luther Harris …

HYDE stares at VANESSA.

CUT TO: "POP'S CORNER" – a music shop on Tottenham
Court Road.

The shop is devoted entirely to the selling of musical
instruments and records: the walls are decorated with the
sleeves of numerous L.P. discs. The discs are on tables and
shelves and several teenage youths are examining the labels
and listening to the background music. There are several
turntables, private listening booths and a small desk complete
with a stool and a cash register.

*The proprietor of the shop – LUTHER HARRIS – sits on the
stool reading a novel. RUTH enters and ignoring LUTHER
crosses to the collection of L.P.s marked "Classical". She
starts looking through the sleeves. After a moment, LUTHER
glances up and recognises RUTH. He climbs down from the
stool and joins her at the table.*

LUTHER: Can I help you, Miss Sanders?

RUTH: Oh – hello! (*Suddenly surprised*) Good
           heavens, is this your shop?

LUTHER: Yes, I'm afraid it is.

RUTH: (*Laughing*) Well, I never! I'm sorry, but I
           didn't realise where I was. I'm on my way to
           a party and I've suddenly discovered it's the
           young man's birthday.

LUTHER: What does your friend like?

RUTH: Oh – he's terribly highbrow …

LUTHER: Does he like Stravinsky?

RUTH: Er – yes, I think so.

*LUTHER starts to look through the selection of classical
discs.*

LUTHER: How's Mr Martin keeping?

RUTH: Oh, he's not too bad, considering. The police have been making rather a nuisance of themselves though.

RUTH's manner is a carefully prepared one; friendly, chatty.

LUTHER: The police?

RUTH: Yes, they keep coming to the studio, and asking the same absurd questions over and over again. It seems to have got worse since that man Talbot was murdered.

LUTHER: Talbot?

RUTH: Yes, he worked for Mrs Curtis, the woman at the hotel …

LUTHER: (*Taking a record from a box*) Which hotel is that?

RUTH: Why, the one at Maidenhead, of course – where Phil was found …

LUTHER: What happened to Talbot?

RUTH: He was murdered – beaten up by someone. But you must have read about it, surely – it was in all the papers?

LUTHER: No, I don't think I did.

RUTH: Well, the police seem to think that Talbot, Philip Martin, and a man called Fletcher were mixed up in a German bank robbery. According to what I've heard the money's still missing.

LUTHER: And does the Inspector think that Larry had anything to do with all this?

RUTH: I don't know; that's what I can't make out. All I know is, they keep interrupting our work. It's absolutely maddening. Hyde came round this morning and questioned Larry for almost an hour.

LUTHER: Almost an hour? Good heavens above …

RUTH: The Inspector's working on a code or other – something to do with photographs and a key. It's

166

all tied up with this search for the money, of course. (*Indicates the record in Luther's hand*) Do you think I could hear that?

LUTHER: (*Pleasantly*) Yes, of course … (*Crosses to one of the turntables*) I shouldn't worry about Larry. I imagine Hyde just wanted his opinion of the photographs.

LUTHER places the record on the turntable and switches on the instrument.

RUTH: I don't know … He kept asking him questions about Arundel most of the time.

LUTHER looks at RUTH.

RUTH: What was he doing at the antique shop? … How many times did he go there? … What was he looking for? … The same dreary old questions … Whether they think the money's hidden away in some …

Suddenly changing the subject, and indicating the turntable.

RUTH: Does that take long to warm up?

LUTHER: No …. No, you'll hear it in a second … I think your friend will like this.

The music starts. LUTHER smiles at RUTH and she smiles back at him.

CUT TO: A mews garage.

LUTHER HARRIS closes the doors of a lock-up garage. He moves to a Ford Zephyr, gets into it, starts up and drives out of the mews.

CUT TO: A main road with an entrance to the mews. *LUTHER drives his car out of the mews onto the main road. CLIFF FLETCHER is sitting in a parked sports car, alone – waiting for LUTHER. As LUTHER drives away, FLETCHER starts up his car and follows LUTHER in pursuit.*

CUT TO: The A284 road.
LUTHER's car is speeding along the road heading to Arundel.

CUT TO: A street near Quayle's antique shop in Arundel. *LUTHER's car draws up to the kerb. LUTHER gets out of the car and looks up and down the deserted street, then closes the car door and strolls towards the street corner. He walks round the corner and looks cautiously down the street, then crosses towards the antique shop which can be seen on the other side of the road. LUTHER crosses and stops at the top of the stairs, looks quickly round up and down the street again then hurries down the steps, taking a key from his pocket. He opens the door leading to the basement and goes in.*

CUT TO: The basement of Quayle's antique shop. *LUTHER closes the door and looks impatiently around the room. He has obviously searched this room very thoroughly before and is looking for new possibilities of a hiding place. He goes quickly to a wall and takes down a picture, looking at the wall behind it. He does this with two more pictures, but with no success. He flings the last picture angrily aside and moves to the door leading to the stairs inside the shop. He hesitates, appearing to hear something. He glances in the direction of the other door, the one leading to the steps to the street. He moves stealthily to the window. He peers out of the window. It is apparently a false alarm. He sighs relievedly and moves quickly to the inner door.*

CUT TO: The basement steps of Quayle's antique shop. *CLIFF FLETCHER is standing flat against the wall, to the extreme right of the basement window – which is why LUTHER hadn't seen him. After a moment he slowly, cautiously, moves toward the entrance to the basement.*

CUT TO: Quayle's Antique Shop.

There are no lights switched on in the shop and the only light comes from the street through the shop windows.

LUTHER is still searching for the money. He has just finished looking in the drawers of an antique desk and, finding nothing in them, slams one of the drawers onto the floor. He suddenly   remembers the fact that he might be seen through the shop window and glances anxiously in their direction. He looks around the shop. Wondering where to look next, he is at his wit's end now. His eyes alight on a large object in a corner of the room, covered by a faded tapestry. He pulls the tapestry aside to reveal the chest. He stares down at the painted lid – then tries unsuccessfully to raise it. The chest is locked. LUTHER is excited now, convinced that he has finally found the money. He looks towards Quayle's desk, goes to it, takes up a steel paper knife and returns to the chest. He bends over it and is about to insert the knife into the lock when a noise from the basement attracts his attention.

CUT TO: The   basement   of   Quayle's   antique   shop.
FLETCHER has just entered from outside and stands near the closed door, his eyes fixed warily on the door leading to the shop stairs. He takes an automatic from his pocket and moves stealthily to the door.

CUT TO: Quayle's Antique Shop.
LUTHER, the knife still in his hand, stands in a listening attitude. He moves quickly and silently to the doorway, awaiting FLETCHER's arrival. FLETCHER appears at the top of the stairs, he pauses there for a moment looking into the shop.

FLETCHER: Luther? … Luther, listen, I know you're here. I
                      followed you down from Town … Look, don't

be a damn fool – if the money's here don't let's waste time fighting. Fifty-fifty – what do you say?

There's no reply. LUTHER waits at the side of the door, then raises the knife ready to strike. FLETCHER looks puzzled now. He comes through the doorway. LUTHER strikes and stabs FLETCHER in the back. FLETCHER gives a strangled cry, the automatic clatters to the shop floor. LUTHER looks on dispassionately as FLETCHER pitches forwards, striking a wardrobe and sliding down it to the floor. LUTHER, pressed for time now, goes frantically into action. He is convinced the money is in the chest. He goes to the chest and starts to work on the lock, at the same time trying to force open the lid. His movements become more and more frenzied. Suddenly, the top part of the chest breaks opens and LUTHER peers inside – it is obvious from his expression that the chest is empty. There is the sound of a car drawing up outside. LUTHER looks in the direction of the shop window with sudden concern.

CUT TO: Outside of Quayle's Antique Shop.
A police car draws up and LARRY, HYDE and two PLAIN CLOTHES MEN get out of the car. HYDE and his party move towards the shop door.

CUT TO: Quayle's Antique Shop.
LUTHER runs towards the doorway leading to the stairway to the basement. A moment later HYDE and his men burst in at the front door of the shop. LARRY is no longer with them. The police look quickly around. One sees the doorway at the back of the shop.
PLAIN CLOTHES MAN: Over here, sir!
They go quickly to the doorway.

CUT TO: The basement of Quayle's Antique Shop. *LUTHER comes through the doorway after running down the stairs from the interior of the shop and crosses to the door leading to the street. He opens it and carefully goes out.*

CUT TO: Outside of Quayle's Antique Shop. *A second police car arrives. INSPECTOR LANG and two PLAIN CLOTHES MEN get out and move quickly to the shop. As they reach it, LUTHER HARRIS comes up the basement steps and walks carefully across the road. As he reaches the corner, he looks back. HYDE is in the doorway and the police are coming up the basement steps. They see HARRIS and give chase. He runs round the corner.*

CUT TO: A street near Quayle's Antique Shop. *LUTHER turns the corner and runs towards his parked car. He opens the door as police appear in the background. He is about to jump in the car, when he stops dead. LARRY is sitting in the passenger seat – he has a revolver in his hand and is pointing it at LUTHER.*

LARRY: What's the hurry, Luther?

From the background we hear the sound of footsteps approaching.

CUT TO: QUAYLE's Antique Shop. *HYDE, INSPECTOR LANG, and a PLAIN CLOTHES SERGEANT called BELLAMY, are examining the empty chest. The sides of the chest have now been broken open revealing a false bottom. As HYDE straightens himself, he looks distinctly annoyed. LARRY sits on the arm of a chair watching them.*

LARRY: You think someone got here ahead of Luther?

HYDE: What do you think, Mr Martin?

BELLAMY: (*To LARRY*) There's a false bottom to the chest so obviously the money was …

HYDE: (*Interrupting him*) It's no good telling us that now! That should have been spotted the day Quayle was murdered!

BELLAMY: (*Defending himself*) The chest appeared to be empty, sir, and since we didn't know about the money then we thought …

HYDE: I know what you thought. Sergeant – that's what I'm complaining about!

LANG: (*To BELLAMY*) We slipped up – there's no other bloody way of looking at it … We just slipped up! (*To HYDE*) I'm sorry, Hyde, but these things happen.

HYDE: And always to me! (*A shrug*) Well – we'll just have to wait and see what happens. Let's hope our friend decides to make a dash for it. (*He looks at his watch*)

CUT TO: A railway platform at Dover.
"The Golden Arrow" arrives and passengers alight. HYDE and a PLAIN CLOTHES SERGEANT can be seen in the background scanning the faces of the passengers.

CUT TO: Emigration Hall, Dover.
Passengers are presenting their passports to a young official who stands behind a narrow desk.

CUT TO: Dockside, Dover.
"The Golden Arrow" passengers have left the emigration hall and are approaching the cross-channel steamer. A group of passengers reach the gangplank and produce their boarding cards. As a tall man reaches the gangplank two men – HYDE and the PLAIN CLOTHES SERGEANT approach him.

HYDE: Excuse me, sir, do you mind coming with us?
TALL MAN: Why should I?
HYDE: I think you know why, Mr Talbot.
BELLAMY takes possession of the suitcase DOUGLAS TALBOT is carrying. TALBOT looks surprised and frightened.

CUT TO: The hall and living room of LARRY MARTIN's flat.
HYDE is sitting on the settee, finishing a whisky and soda. RUTH, LARRY and the INSPECTOR have been discussing the events of the past few days.

HYDE: … It was Talbot, of course, that changed the photograph in the show case. He knew that we were suspicious of you and would become even more so, once we discovered that you had apparently taken the pictures in the first place. It was to Talbot's advantage to discredit your story and throw as much suspicion onto you as possible.

LARRY: When did you first suspect that the dead man wasn't Talbot?

HYDE: The diary made me suspicious. I couldn't believe that Fletcher would have left it in Talbot's pocket. Then shortly after the murder was committed a report came through that a farm worker was missing – I put two and two together.

RUTH: Was it Talbot that left the suitcase at Victoria?

HYDE: No, that was Luther Harris. He'd double-crossed   his colleagues and helped himself to part of the loot. Later he became frightened and decided to use the money to divert

173

suspicion from himself. (*Placing the empty glass on the table*) He couldn't imagine anyone suspecting him after he'd handed over the suitcase.

RUTH: And Dr Linderhof – how does he fit into all this?

HYDE smiles at RUTH as he rises from the settee.

HYDE: He didn't. He just happened to overhear the conversation between Mrs Curtis and Philip Martin. Of course, we had our eyes on Linderhof at one time – (*Smiling at LARRY*) We had our eye on everyone if it comes to that. Talbot knew this of course and deliberately fostered the impression that Linderhof was in league with you.

RUTH: What happened to Dr Linderhof? Wasn't he in trouble with the medical authorities?

HYDE: Yes. The case came up two days ago. He was completely exonerated. I understand he's started practising again. (*Holding out his hand to LARRY*) Mr Martin – thank you for all your help. I'm more than grateful.

LARRY: (*Shaking hands with HYDE*) Thank you, Inspector.

HYDE: Goodbye, Miss Sanders. If you ever get tired of Mr Martin give me a ring. After the help you gave us with Luther Harris we can always find a place for you at Scotland Yard.

RUTH: (*Laughing*) Thank you, Inspector.

HYDE goes out into the hall with LARRY. RUTH collects the glasses from the table and crosses to her desk. After a moment we hear the front door close, then LARRY returns. He looks

*thoughtful, preoccupied, as he moves down to the settee.
RUTH watches him for a moment.*

RUTH: What are you thinking about?

LARRY turns and faces RUTH.

RUTH: Your brother?

LARRY: Yes.

RUTH moves closer to LARRY.

RUTH: Don't, Larry – please don't … Try not to think
             about him … There's an awful lot of work to do,
             you know – you've been neglecting things just
             recently.

LARRY: Yes, I suppose I have. (*He smiles at RUTH*) Well
             – after dinner we'll really get down to it.

RUTH: (*Surprised*) After dinner?

LARRY: Yes. (*He looks at his watch*) I booked the table for
             eight o'clock. It's time we left.

RUTH: We?

LARRY: That's right. We. Us. It's "Be Nice To Your
             Secretary Week", Miss Sanders – didn't you
             know?

RUTH: No, I didn't, Mr Martin – but I'm all for it.

*LARRY laughs and then suddenly taking hold of RUTH's arm
he draws her gently towards him.*

THE END

Press Pack

Press cuttings about *The Desperate People* ...

Francis Durbridge introduces his new six-part thriller serial

A considerable responsibility always rests upon the shoulders of an actor picked to play the lead in a television serial. He must have an arresting personality and be able to keep an audience's attention from one episode to the next, usually through wildly different situations. It is understandable, therefore, that a writer is always on the look out for an actor to tackle this demanding role.

When I was in New York almost two years ago I was very impressed by the performance of Denis Quilley in the Broadway production of the musical play *Irma La Douce.* I wrote to Alan Bromly – the producer of my tv serials – a letter saying how much I had enjoyed Quilley's performance and what an excellent leading man he would make for one of my future serials. Having completed *The Desperate People* at the end of 1962 I was delighted to learn that Quilley was now in England, and was indeed thinking of once again playing a straight part in a completely different type of entertainment.

The Desperate People is a fast-moving action-suspense thriller story in six episodes and does not feature either Tim Frazer or that even better known character Paul Temple who appears in my radio serials.

Larry Martin, the main character in the story, is a professional photographer who earns his living by photographing beautiful girls for magazines and commercial advertisements.

Larry becomes involved in a series of exciting events following the appearance of his younger brother, Philip, on leave from the army. The story unfolds against a typical

English background and much of the location filming was done in and around the delightful town of Arundel in Sussex.

During the showing of my previous serials, I have frequently received letters from viewers complaining that they have missed a particular episode, and would I be kind enough to send them a detailed synopsis of the episode in question! On one occasion I even had to cable the denouement of one of my serials to a family on the way to Australia.

The Desperate People, however, is being screened at a time when the whole family should be able to watch every episode of the entire serial – Sunday afternoon. This time is considered to be ideal for serial viewers.

Although I try to make each serial of mine as different as possible, I am confident that if you enjoyed my previous serials *The Scarf, A Time of Day, The World of Tim Frazer*, and so on, you will enjoy following the adventures of *The Desperate People* right through to the last episode.

The Return of Durbridge by John Chelsfield

The man who made the first big impact of a writer of thriller serials, Francis Durbridge, is back in the business again. *The Desperate People*, the BBC's new six-part thriller which starts tomorrow afternoon, is his tenth.

Durbridge serials have always enjoyed great success, and for very good reasons. He has a flair for projecting the conventional whodunnit patterns against new and intriguing backgrounds.

His characters are boldly drawn. The outlines are strong and impressive, but there is nothing too complicated inside. A cynic might say that some of Durbridge's characters have come straight out of the filing cabinet, with a change of name for each new story. But I think this would be an unfair criticism.

Durbridge thickens his plot with a great diversity of boldly-labelled characters in much the same way that Edgar Wallace used to. Up to the last chapter or the last episode the villain of the piece could be anyone of half-a-dozen or more characters.

The viewer is kept in suspense until the last possible moment. In fact Durbridge goes one better than that. Even the members of the cast of his serials are kept in the dark about the identity of the villain – right up to rehearsals of the final episode.

It is a formula well suited to television's mass audience. This is the television application of the pure whodunnit technique. Durbridge employs it with greater skill than is sometimes apparent. Escapist entertainment, with a veneer of sophistication is the aim, rather than harsh realism.

Some of Durbridge's serials have found favour with overseas audiences. The last one he did for BBC *The World of Tim Frazer* – this one ran to eighteen episodes – has just been shown in Germany and is now running on Telefis Eireann with considerable success.

Tomorrow's new serial concerns mysterious events in the wake of the death of an Army man in a hit-and-run accident.

For Durbridge fans, his earlier successes were: *The Broken Horseshoe* (1952), *Operation Diplomat* (1952), *The Teckman Biography* (1953), *The Portrait of Alison* (1955), *My Friend Charles* (1956), *The Other Man* (1956), *A Time of Day* (1957) and *The Scarf* (1959).

Liverpool Daily Post

Now We Can Play Murder At Tea-Time by **Fred Cooke**
Herrings for Sunday tea. The reddest, as supplied by Francis Durbridge. His *The Desperate People* introduces something new to the British Sunday afternoon way of life. Hunt-the-murderer has now become a game all the family can play.

179

Durbridge is so prolific with his characters, dead and alive, that no matter how many fall by the wayside, he usually finishes up with as many as he started with.

Some have no other purpose than to throw us off the scent. But when the end comes after six instalments all will have pulled their weight.

Durbridge seems to have gone in for a new-style hero. Jack Hedley's Tim Frazer shrieked "hero" from the first corpse.

But if Denis Quilley hadn't been quickly labelled as the one character beyond suspicion (I think), I'd have added him to my list of suspects.

Earlier Durbridge serials are selling well overseas. From Germany comes the story of the cinema chief so alarmed at the *The Scarf* affecting audiences that he gave away the plot of the final episode. A dirty trick, but a handsome tribute to Durbridge.

Sunday Citizen

Durbridge's Wide Appeal by Robert G. Archer

The Desperate People, starting tomorrow evening, is Francis Durbridge's tenth BBC TVs thriller serial, and the seventh produced by Alan Bromly. Many of these serials have been seen abroad. Feelings ran high among German viewers when a cinema executive deliberately gave away the plot of the final episode of *The Scarf* which, he claimed, was keeping people away from his cinema.

Durbridge's most recent serial, the eighteen-part *The World of Tim Frazer*, has been shown in Germany and is now being shown on Telefís Eireann, where it is winning high praise from press and public. With *The Desperate People* he returns to the format of the single adventure in six weekly episodes, used in all his previous serials. The Durbridge tradition of keeping the cast in the dark about the identity of the villain is preserved.

The thriller concerns Larry Martin, a successful commercial photographer, who has a younger brother, Philip, serving in the British Army in Germany. Philip returns to spend some leave with his elder brother in London but explains that first he has to go to Ireland to see the widow of an army friend, killed recently by a hit-and-run driver. After Philip has left him, Larry discovers his brother has been lying to him. When he attempts to discover the reason for this, he finds himself getting involved with a shadowy group of people who will use any means to stop him from getting to the truth.

Larry Martin is played by Denis Quilley, Renny Lister plays Larry's secretary Ruth Sanders, and Hugh Cross is cast as Inspector Hyde.

Rochdale Observer

The Desperate People Episode 2
In tonight's second episode of the new Francis Durbridge thriller-serial Larry Martin's enquiries into the death of his brother Philip are taking him ever further away from his life as a professional photographer. Philip, a serving soldier in Germany, had arrived home to spend leave with Larry, but left almost immediately – apparently for Dublin. A service friend, Sean Reynolds, had been killed in a Hamburg car accident – and he wanted to see the man's widow. But Philip never reached Dublin; instead, he was found dead in a hotel near Maidenhead – seemingly by his own hand.

Larry (Denis Quilley) cannot accept the verdict of suicide, particularly because of the strange business of the photographs: he has received through the post a portrait of Philip which used to be on display in the showcase outside his own studio. And in its place he has found – a picture of the mysterious Sean Reynolds and his wife …

Radio Times

Reviews

Hokum As Usual, But It's Fun by **Dennis Potter**

A well-done television thriller, lovingly garnished with cleverly cooked clues and topped with dark hints of mystery, is particularly appetising at Sunday tea-time.

Yesterday the BBC began the first instalment of a six-part serial, freshly and crisply baked by that accomplished suspense-monger Francis Durbridge.

The Desperate People was excellent fare, and the stock ingredients of the whodunnit oozed out like jam from a squashed doughnut.

Already a young soldier on leave has been found dead in his room at an hotel. He has left a note for his brother and the police call it suicide.

Durbridge addicts know better. The brother, played with craggy determination by Denis Quilley, refuses to accept such an explanation.

The great merit of hokum like this lies in the complete lack of pretension and the cunning professionalism of the script.

All Mr Durbridge's dialogue is designed to provoke action and puzzled apprehension. It is so urgently composed that we are never given a moment to ponder upon the implausibilities.

Daily Herald

The new Francis Durbridge serial on BBC TV got off to a good start on Sunday (February 24) and he is certain to keep his fans happy and guessing for the next five episodes. It is screened at a suitable time for all the family (4.55) and if the first episode is any indication it should be another winner for Mr Durbridge.

A young soldier's suicide, the murder of his best friend, a mysterious German doctor and a disappearing photograph which looks like a vital clue, all the ingredients were immediately introduced and episode one got right down to cases.

Denis Quilley plays the young photographer whose brother commits suicide, Hugh Cross the detective-inspector and Gerard Heinz the German doctor.

Television Today

An exciting initial impression was made by *The Desperate People,* the new thriller serial by that master of the question mark Francis Durbridge. No disappointment here – but Sunday afternoon means that a lot of people are not going to see all the episodes.

This is Durbridge's tenth thriller, but it was quickly apparent that he had lost none of his ability to intrigue and tease viewers.

The story moved smartly to the meat of the mystery – the inexplicable suicide of a young British soldier on leave and the baffling complications were cleverly introduced.

My guess is that in the Durbridge tradition *The Desperate People* will keep us engaged happily in conjecture until the final episode – if we are free on Sundays at the curiously chosen time of 4.55pm.

Hanley Evening Sentinel

Francis Durbridge's BBC serial *The Desperate People* gets more engrossing each week.

This brisk thriller has all the ingredients to keep one guessing. There are suspects galore (always a new one to

183

replace those who get bumped off), false trails and a cliff hanger technique which defies you to miss the next episode.

Sheffield Star

The Francis Durbridge thriller serial *The Desperate People* pursues its inevitable course of mystery, tension and murder. His characters are polished and polite, his plot is ingeniously contrived and Alan Bromly's production is slick.

The combination of these two masters of their craft weaves a spell over me. Once I start watching a Durbridge story I must see it through. This is Durbridge's tenth serial for the BBC. The magic is still as potent as ever.

The Desperate People will probably do as much for Denis Quilley (who plays the hero) as *The World of Tim Frazer* did for Jack Hedley.

Yorkshire Evening Post

The Desperate People (BBC Sunday) has followed up one of the best opening instalments of a mystery series with a quietly mounting tension in the familiar Francis Durbridge manner. It looks as if we are in for some gripping cloak-and-dagger stuff before we learn the identity of that mysterious Dublin couple.

Irish Independent

The Francis Durbridge serial *The Desperate People* promises to live up to the reputation of the previous thrillers by this writer.

It keeps the tension stretched taut all the time, and also interests one in the various characters.

Denis Quilley, the main character, is involved in the mystery of the behaviour and death of his brother. He is an actor who looks as though he may make as strong an impact, in a different manner, as Jack Hedley as Tim Frazer.

I also look forward to seeing more of Renny Lister, who plays his secretary Ruth Sanders. Here is an interesting young actress who can give vitality to the smallest scene.

Newcastle-on-Tyne Evening Chronicle

The Desperate People Episode 4

Photographer Larry Martin, the man at the centre of this Francis Durbridge thriller serial, tonight continues his quest for the truth about his soldier brother's death. He has come by a key, found among his brother's effects, but is it the key to the mystery? His unknown adversaries certainly seem to think so, judging by their efforts to take it away from him. However, their last attempt to do so has instead left Larry in possession of another clue – a ticket for a dance. And that is why in tonight's episode Larry (Denis Quilley) and his secretary go dancing – and meet the Stansdales, a couple whose faces seem very familiar ...

Radio Times

Letter From A Viewer

The Desperate People : We are indeed desperate – to find out what will happen next week. For sheer "cliff-hanging" episodes Francis Durbridge has 'em all beaten. Roll on 4.55 this afternoon.

Glasgow Sunday Mail